MW00936708

A RISK WORTH TAKING

A RED RIVER NOVEL

VICTORIA JAMES

This book is a work of fiction. Names, characters, places, and incidents are the product of the author's imagination or are used fictitiously. Any resemblance to actual events, locales, or persons, living or dead, is coincidental.

Copyright © 2013 by Victoria James. All rights reserved, including the right to reproduce, distribute, or transmit in any form or by any means. For information regarding subsidiary rights, please contact the Publisher.

Entangled Publishing, LLC
2614 South Timberline Road
Suite 109
Fort Collins, CO 80525
Visit our website at www.entangledpublishing.com.

Bliss is an imprint of Entangled Publishing, LLC. For more information on our titles, visit http://www.entangledpublishing.com/category/bliss

Edited by Karen Grove and Wendy Chen
Cover design by Jessica Cantor

ISBN 978-1-50281-379-4

Manufactured in the United States of America

First Edition March 2013

Bliss

Thank you to my parents, who showed me the power of unconditional love—and showed me the value in not taking the road most traveled.
Love you always.

Prologue

Holly Carrington had been waiting precisely six years and four months for this day.

She was about to get the promotion she had worked her butt off for. She could feel it down to the tips of her toes, which were, at the moment, painfully encased in chocolate-brown leather, three-inch, high-heeled boots purchased specifically for this occasion—and with a blasphemous disregard for comfort.

Holly's back stiffened and she scooted a little closer to the edge of her chair as the large glass doors to Martin Laurence's office opened with a familiar, forceful swoosh. Martin Laurence, the founder and visionary behind the country's preeminent interior design house, had entered the room. Holly knew from the moment she had graduated six years ago that she wanted to work for him. Only the best got hired, and only the most exceptional and diligent lasted at his firm. Once hired, her next goal had been to make senior

$\mathcal{A}$ $\mathcal{R}$ISK $\mathcal{W}$ORTH $\mathcal{T}$AKING

designer before the age of thirty.

The scent of Martin's pleasant, fresh cologne wafted through the air as he walked by her, his Italian leather loafers echoing on the gleaming marble floor. Holly's eyes followed him as he gracefully sank into the plush chair behind his massive glass and steel desk and smiled at her.

"Good morning, Holly," Martin said smoothly, his blue eyes locking onto hers.

"Good morning, Martin," she replied with as much composure as she could manage.

"Holly, I'm not going to beat around the bush, you and I are both too busy for that. I think you know why you're here this morning. From day one you have been an asset to this firm. Your dedication, your designs, and your attitude have always made you stand out. I had you pegged for excellence the moment you started here, and you haven't let me down once. I'm so pleased to offer you the position of Senior Designer," he said, finishing with his wide, perfectly polished smile.

It took two seconds for his words to sink in, and then Holly felt the rush of accomplishment engulf her. She wanted to jump out of her leather club chair and scream *YES!* at the top of her lungs. She settled on a controlled, perfectly acceptable squeal of delight and tapped her feet on the floor. Martin indulged her by laughing.

"Martin, thank you *so* much. You have no idea what this means to me. This has been my dream since I started working here. When you hired me, I was intimidated by the talent, but so determined to show you that I could succeed. It has been an honor to work with you, and I've learned so much," she said, her words tumbling out of her mouth.

"Thank you, Holly. I don't ever remember hiring someone with such a work ethic. Your designs are fabulous, and our clients love you."

Holly waved a slender hand, graciously brushing off the compliment. But inside she cherished his words—Martin didn't hand out praise very often.

"I'd also like to take this opportunity to go over your new responsibilities, expectations, and, of course, salary and bonus packages," Martin said, his eyes twinkling as he slid a black leather portfolio across the desk.

Holly couldn't stop smiling as she reached for the folder, her perfect French-manicured nails standing out against the black leather. Poor, small-town Holly was no more. She had been replaced by this successful, confident, twenty-eight-year-old woman who had made a name for herself in a cut-throat business. Tonight she was going to celebrate with her sister, Jennifer, her brother-in-law, and their six-month-old daughter. The timing couldn't have been better. Jen had invited Holly to dinner tonight, and Holly was going to surprise them with the drawings and plans she had just completed for their home renovation. In a few months, Jen and Rick were going to be leaving the city behind to move back to their hometown of Red River. Holly and Jen had inherited their grandparents' old home—and it had always been Jen's dream to live there again. Holly was looking forward to heading up the renovation for them and had already secured a leave of absence to oversee the project. She and Jennifer had come a long way together, and there wasn't anyone more deserving of that home.

The low vibration of a cell phone against Martin's glass desktop yanked Holly from her thoughts, and both she

and Martin glanced to see which phone was buzzing. Sure enough, it was hers.

"If you have to answer that, go ahead," Martin said, motioning with his chin to her phone. Keeping their high-profile, high-maintenance clients happy was a priority. Holly nodded, her finger already on the button to accept the call.

"Holly Carrington, senior designer at the Martin Group," she answered in a singsong voice. Martin chuckled and shifted away from her to look at his computer.

There was brief static on the other end of the line and then, "Holly Carrington?"

"Yes," Holly replied, her smile faltering marginally at the woman's tight, clipped tone.

"Ms. Carrington, my name is Kathleen and I'm a nurse at Toronto General Hospital."

Holly frowned, her mind scurrying for a reason that the hospital would be calling her.

"I'm sorry, Ms. Carrington, but your sister, Jennifer, has been involved in a car accident."

Holly's heart lurched forward. "Car accident?"

"Yes, Ms. Carrington. I'm afraid we need you to get to the hospital as soon as possible. Your sister and her husband were badly injured," the nurse said, her tone softening.

The impact of those words hit Holly with the force of a falling building. She didn't move. She stared at Martin's perfectly coiffed black hair. His pleasant, expensive cologne had suddenly become overpowering and stifling. The low rumble of traffic below, the honking horns, and muted pe-destrian chatter circled around her. She could not process. Could not breathe. Could not speak.

"Ms. Carrington, are you still there?"

Holly bit her lower lip, feeling the sting of blood creep into her mouth. She cleared her throat and forced out the only question that mattered. "Are they okay?"

The nurse sighed. "Ms. Carrington, I wish it were better news. We will tell you everything when you get here. Are you able to get to the hospital?"

"Yes, of course," Holly murmured, standing, adrenaline finally kicking in as she scrambled with hands that felt like rubber to gather her belongings. She needed to get to her family.

"Come to the Emergency Department. Identify yourself, and you'll be escorted inside."

Holly stopped abruptly, her bag dropping to the ground with a loud thud as a chilling thought stole through her.

Holly asked a question that her heart already had the answer to. She asked it with a voice she didn't recognize, and with a heart that was breaking. "But they are going to be okay? My sister is going to be okay, right?"

"I'm so sorry, Ms. Carrington."

The tremor that began in her heart exploded like a bomb throughout her core, consuming everything inside her as the voice on the other end confirmed news she would never be able to accept.

Slowly, the carefully put together ensemble consisting of a new silk suit, matching chocolate brown leather boots, perfectly highlighted caramel-colored hair, and meticulously applied makeup began to feel as though it were being peeled, pulled, and stripped from her body.

All of it superficial, unimportant trivialities.

Chapter One

"Daniel, this is my first day off work, remember? My high-maintenance clients are now yours. Enjoy," Holly teased, her eyes focused on the country road ahead. "I know it'll be boring over there without me for two months, but I'll be back," she promised, her smile wavering as the "Welcome to Red River" sign came into view. The blue, wooden billboard was a little weathered, a little beaten, but it was achingly familiar.

"I'm sure I'll manage. But first, you need to give me your opinion on that color," Daniel whined.

Holly didn't answer him. The jolt of sentimentality that clogged her throat as she approached her hometown rendered her incapable of giving a damn which shade of taupe paint should be used in the Thorntons' front foyer. "I'm sorry to cut you off, but I'm going to have to call you back," Holly whispered, not waiting for her colleague's response. She threw her hands-free earpiece onto the empty passenger seat beside her.

Holly eased her foot off the gas, allowing her life in the city to fade away as she entered the town she hadn't called home for ten years. A barrage of memories she didn't even know she possessed pummeled through her tired mind and hijacked her senses as she drove down the hill she and Jennifer had once bicycled on daily as children. She wondered if it still smelled of fresh-cut grass and dewy fall leaves. The old lift-bridge looked the same, but the view was different from her SUV.

Holly almost missed the turn onto the road that led to her grandparents' vacant house. Her sweating hands gripped the leather steering wheel and her stomach turned at a nauseating pace as the faded yellow-brick Victorian home came into view. It was no longer the same majestic, proud structure it had been when her grandparents were alive. Instead, it was a sorry shell of the house that once was.

The grass that her grandfather had meticulously cut every week was now knee high and unkempt. Her grandmother's spotless veranda looked more brown than white. And it didn't look nearly as welcoming without the overflowing flower baskets that her grandmother had hung at every post on the porch. The bright yellow watering can she so clearly remembered from her youth wasn't on the ledge, and the white wicker furniture was in storage. Holly frowned as she stared at the sight before her. The property was achingly deserted. If a house could have shed tears, this one surely would have. Neither she nor Jen had the heart to sell their childhood home after their grandparents had died, especially since Jen had always made it clear that when she had a family, she'd move back to Red River. It should have been the four of them driving here today, ready to embark on the renovation. It was Jen's dream to return the old house to its former glory, and to have Ella's laughter filling the rooms, just as Jen's and Holly's had done so long ago. Except things hadn't gone according to plan. Jen had never even seen Holly's plans for the home. Now Jen and Rick were gone…

Ella's gentle snore from the backseat forced Holly to get a grip on her emotions. She clutched the steering wheel tightly, her knuckles turning white. She needed to remember why she was here—renovate, decorate, and sell the house. Then all her ties to this town would be permanently severed. She wouldn't be forced to remember all the people she'd lost. She wouldn't have to fight the images of them when they'd all been alive and living here together. Eight weeks. She had to survive eight weeks in Red River, and then she could get back to her regularly scheduled life in Toronto.

Holly turned onto the long, gravel-filled driveway lined with evergreens and parked in front of the detached garage. She glanced over her shoulder at Ella, who was still sleeping peacefully, her lips hugging the pacifier. Holly pulled her keys out of the ignition and eyed the distance from the front porch to her SUV. She decided she could safely leave Ella in the car while she opened up the house. Ella had only fallen asleep twenty minutes ago, and she had no intention of waking her, especially since the baby wouldn't be able to nap until Holly figured out how to assemble the crib. Ella's nanny, Mary, had emphasized repeatedly the importance of Ella having a daily nap. Holly wished that Mary could have made the trip with them, but it was against agency policy. So now Holly was about to have a crash-course in dealing with her little niece—and it terrified her. Back in Toronto, Mary had done all the day-to-day caregiving, while Holly maintained her grueling work schedule. Now it was all up to Holly. She glanced over at Ella one more time, made sure the back window was open slightly, then quietly stepped from the driver's seat, locking the car after she'd shut the door.

Her running shoes crunched softly against the gravel as she walked up the uneven path to the porch. Images flashed before her eyes: her grandfather mowing the lawn, her grandmother standing with the door ajar, calling them in for dinner, while she and Jennifer chattered about the latest school gossip on the front porch. If she could just have one more minute with them, one moment to tell them how much she loved them and to feel the warmth of their hugs… She refused to let the tears that were incessantly filling her eyes fall. But oh, she wanted a good, long cry. She wanted to weep for the couple that had given her courage and love and strength, and cry for the sister that she missed every single day. She cleared her throat and shook her head. *Get a hold of yourself, Holly.* She buttoned her chunky sweater coat with a slight shiver, the damp fall air adding to the chills that were already weaving through her body as she made her way to the front porch. There were boards covering the windows and front door. She knew she was early, but she had hoped that Quinn would have gotten around to opening up the house for her. She'd obviously thought wrong.

The smooth, low rumble of a car engine approaching ripped through the silence of her thoughts. A black Range Rover crunched against gravel and rolled to a smooth stop behind her SUV. Her heart picked up pace because she already knew who was in that vehicle.

Holly had contacted Quinn Manning months ago, letting him know that she was coming back to Red River and

needed his company to handle the restoration and renovation of her grandparents' house. She had no choice but to
contact Manning & Son Construction: they were the best
renovation and building company around. And despite the
many passing years, her stomach still did a few traitorous
somersaults and her heart skipped when Quinn's deep voice
had greeted hers on the other end of the line. And then her
mind had gone to her last night in Red River—when she'd
humiliated herself in front of the man. Of course, she knew
Quinn would never bring it up. He had probably dismissed it
as just a silly teenage crush. Better he thought that.

Holly wiped her clammy hands on the front of her jeans
as Quinn approached. This would be the first time she'd seen
him in years… Maybe he'd lost his appeal. Maybe age had
turned him into someone that didn't resemble the young
man she had fantasized about in high school. As Quinn
rounded the corner, her question was answered: unfortu-
nately for her, Quinn had only gotten better looking with
age. A jolt of energy stronger than a grande non-fat cappuc-
cino coursed through her veins. Quinn's face had become
more rugged, his chiseled features more striking—almost as
striking as the blue eyes that were staring at her intently. The
navy crewneck he wore hugged broad, sculpted shoulders
and a flat, narrow waist. His dark blue, faded jeans outlined
his long, powerful legs. With each step he took in her direction, it was as though he erased each year that had passed.
His walk was casual, but so sexy, so confident, so…*Quinn*.
He had the walk of a man who knew himself and didn't give
a damn what the world thought of him.

Holly waved, and then, feeling awkward, quickly put her
hand back down.

"Welcome back, Holly," Quinn said as he reached the front porch. His voice held a note of tenderness, and it ignited a flame in her heart. He perched his right work boot on the first step, his large, tanned hand leaning against his denim-clad leg, and she found herself reacting to the very masculine pose.

"Thanks, it's nice to see you," she answered, trying not to cringe at the awkwardness she heard in her voice.

"You, too," he said, his eyes flickering over her. Holly clutched the corners of her sweater together tightly. *He's not checking you out, he's just, well, looking at a person he hasn't seen in a long time.* Holly wondered what he saw when he looked at her. Gone was the girl from his past, that much was obvious. She wasn't as skinny as she had been at eighteen. She felt old, like she'd aged twenty years in the last four months. And then there was the matter of her weekend "uniform," which consisted of jeans and T-shirts and, if she were lucky, a sweater. Today, she was lucky. And if she grasped the curled edges of said sweater together tightly enough, she might even be able to hide the remainder of Ella's lunch she was sure was crusted on the shirt beneath it. She had no idea how Ella's nanny always seemed so neat and tidy. After only a few minutes with Ella, Holly was always covered in either juice or food.

"I'm so sorry about Jennifer," he said, frowning, his voice gruff with emotion. It was the softness in his deep voice, the empathy she saw in his eyes, that made her breath catch and her heart ache. But she couldn't talk about it. She didn't want to talk about it. Because if she did, she would break down. And she couldn't do that.

"Thank you," she managed to say finally, breaking from

his stare to look down at her muddy running shoes, wanting to look anywhere but at the blue depths of his eyes.

"Holly—"

"You think you can help me get into this place?" she interrupted, nudging her chin toward the house. He stared at her a second longer, then gave a quick nod, the sympathy in his expression intensifying, like he knew that she was trying to change the subject.

"Of course I can. I just got back into town yesterday, or I would have already been over to open this place up." He joined her on the porch and studied the plywood boards blocking the front door. Holly exhaled quietly with relief as he focused his attention on the house.

"You're here early, aren't you?" Quinn asked, his back to her as he tried one of the planks.

"Yeah, I thought I'd get a head start."

"You always were an overachiever," he mumbled, as he tore off one of the boards.

Holly was too distracted to even respond. She was disgusted with herself when an involuntary shiver of awareness teased her as she watched Quinn almost effortlessly place one of the boards beside the door. What was it about this town that brought out all the primal instincts in her? She was a strong, capable, independent woman. Why did the sight of Quinn, in his low-slung, well-worn jeans, prying off a piece of wood, suddenly make her feel feverish? Next thing you knew, she'd be making him dinner and doing his laundry.

Quinn wiped his hands on his jeans and turned around. Holly lifted her eyes in a hurry. She hoped to God he hadn't seen her checking out his butt. His very nice butt. And she wasn't even going to analyze what it meant, that this was the first time in months that she'd noticed a man. She had spent the last four months in a daze, trying to juggle work, Ella, and her grief. But a few seconds back in Quinn's presence, and all her senses were ignited again.

"Thanks, Quinn," she said, clearing her voice.

A faint cry tore Holly from her thoughts. Ella. Holly ran down the walkway to her SUV, pressing the unlock button on her keys right before whipping open Ella's door. Ella's green eyes locked onto hers, and then seconds later she broke into a toothy, slobbery smile. Her round face was pink from her crying, and her brown hair was standing on end, but the sight of Holly calmed her almost instantly. It was a humbling and terrifying feeling, knowing that she could do that, that little Ella had that much faith in her.

Ella and the current state of her SUV was a reflection of her new lifestyle. Once, the black leather seats were gleaming and pristine. Now, the interior was filled with empty coffee cups and stuffed animals, a car seat, a diaper bag, and a crib in a box that she was going to have to assemble before bedtime. There was not one indication that the woman who drove this car had her act together.

Quinn stood beside her without saying a word. She felt the heat emanating off him. He smelled enticing, comforting, sort of like man and nature and...something else that you just couldn't get from a bottle. After all these years, he still had the ability to make her knees weak just by his very proximity. She turned to look up at him, trying to decipher the expression behind the shadows in his eyes.

"This is Ella," she said, looking from the baby to him. Ella was transfixed on Quinn, her bright eyes doing a thorough once-over. She even leaned forward in her car seat and

peered down at his feet.

"Jennifer's daughter?" Quinn asked, his voice thick, strained.

Holly nodded, jamming her hands into the back pockets of her jeans.

"She's beautiful," he said hoarsely, and then surprised her by breaking out in a wide smile for Ella. Ella, it seemed, was enchanted by Quinn, and she let out an exuberant squeal of delight that included arms and legs flailing. It was so contagious, they all laughed.

"That's a pretty name," he said, still smiling.

"I think so," Holly replied softly as she unbuckled Ella, picking her up and perching her on her hip.

"So, want to go inside?" he asked, cocking his head toward the house.

"That would be great," she said truthfully. "I'd really like to get started on the reno as soon as possible." She threw her purse over one shoulder and was about to grab the diaper bag when Quinn interceded, effortlessly taking a piece of luggage from the backseat as well as the diaper bag. *Don't be impressed by that, Holly, he just has manners.*

She followed him up the walkway, holding Ella a little closer, remembering how far they had come. Ella had been miraculously untouched in the accident, remaining in the hospital only one night for observation and testing. The night Holly had brought her home from the hospital had been one of the most surreal, frightening nights in her life. She hadn't turned on any lights when they arrived at her one-bedroom loft, instead letting the Toronto skyline cast its reassuring glow through the windows. She had carefully unbuckled Ella from her carrier and brought her into bed with her. Fear and grief had paralyzed Holly—fear that she wouldn't be good enough for Ella, that she wouldn't be able to cope, to care. Fear that she would never be enough, that she would never be good enough of a parent to replace the ones the little baby had lost. How could she? Jen had always wanted a child, had always wanted to be a mother—and Ella had been their world. The guilt Holly felt for being alive and raising their beloved daughter had threatened to consume her that night. Holly sat on top of the white duvet, her legs crossed, and her bloodshot eyes staring at Ella, flashes of her past playing across the baby's tranquil face. She remembered her mother, her grandparents, her sister, Rick...

How could all the people she'd ever loved be gone?

But somehow she and Ella had made it. They were here. And they'd go on, just the two of them.

"Do you have keys?" Quinn asked when they'd reached the front door. Ella was quiet, looking at the new surroundings, and then staring at Quinn, who was studying the rusting lock.

"Yeah, hold on," Holly murmured, hoping they were in her purse. She shifted Ella to her other hip and tried looking for them in her once-pristine Coach handbag. The designer purse she had purchased for an important lunch meeting with a potential client was now stained, filled with baby wipes, tissues, and an ancient brown banana that she kept forgetting to throw out.

"They're in here somewhere," she mumbled, very aware of Quinn's eyes on her. But that darn banana kept getting in the way. She glanced up and her stomach clenched at the sight of Quinn smiling at Ella.

"Would you mind holding this?" Holly asked, looking

deep into her purse again as she thrust the mushy brown banana in his general direction. Before Quinn could take it from her, Ella intercepted and wrapped her hands around the base of the banana and squeezed so hard that the gooey, wet innards erupted from its brown casing and splattered all over Quinn and Ella.

"Holy f—" Quinn's eyes darted to Ella. "Fudge."

"Omigod, omigod, Quinn. I'm so—"

Holly watched in horror as Ella then smeared the banana on Quinn's face and laughed. Holly couldn't look anymore. She placed Ella on the porch and ducked her head into her purse as she frantically fished out the pack of baby wipes. She didn't look Quinn in the eye as she yanked out a dozen or so moist wipes. How was it possible that she was back in town only minutes and she was already humiliating herself? These things never happened when Mary was around.

"Um, here," Holly choked, stepping closer to Quinn. She focused on the banana chunks on his chin and cheeks rather than his eyes.

Quinn grabbed the wipes from her. "I can clean my face, Holly," he muttered. To her relief, it looked as though he was trying to hold in his laughter. Holly backed up a step and reached down for Ella, who in five seconds had managed to mash the banana into her hair like a deep conditioning treatment. Holly resisted the urge to swear loudly.

Quinn finished wiping his face and shirt while Holly contemplated whether or not she should say something.

"I guess I should clean out my purse more often," Holly said stiffly. For some reason Ella thought that was hilarious and cackled loudly. Quinn looked up and joined her.

Except he didn't cackle. No, he had a rich, deep laugh that made Holly feel warm and tingly. And his eyes still had that twinkle she remembered. Despite the fact that he still had banana stains on the front of his shirt and was holding dirty baby wipes in his hands, Quinn looked about as sexy a man as she'd ever seen. Holly started rummaging again in her purse more furiously, determined to hide her embarrassment and irrational thoughts.

"What else do you have in there?" he asked, peering into her traitorous bag. Ella copied his movement and tried looking into her bag, too, almost overturning herself as the weight of her head lunged her forward.

"Got them!" Holly gasped, dangling the keys in the air triumphantly, just out of Ella's reach. Quinn's lips twitched, his blue eyes sparkling as he took the keys from her hands.

"Thanks," he said as their fingers touched for the briefest of seconds. And there it was: the shivers, the thrill, the buzz that stimulated all her senses and threw her heart into overdrive.

Quinn didn't seem to notice as he was already trying the keys. After jiggling the old lock on the door for a few seconds, he finally swung it open. A cloud of dust greeted them, and Quinn stepped inside, holding the door open and fanning his arm through the cloud.

"Jake said the power should be on." He flicked the light switch beside the door.

Nothing happened.

But Holly wasn't thinking about the electricity. She was being transported back in time. There was enough light streaming through the front door that she could make out the details of the old entryway. It was exactly as she remembered. Except the sweet aroma of her grandmother's baking wasn't here to greet her. And there wasn't a gentle, elderly voice calling out from the kitchen. There was just… quiet. She let her purse slide off her shoulder and gently drop to the ground as she walked further into the foyer.

Holly loved the layout of this home, seeing it for the first time from a designer's perspective. The old house had a center hall plan. There was a large, formal dining room to the left of the entrance, and a large living room to the right. Both rooms had big bay windows with thick-trim detailing and glorious wainscoting. She loved the French doors with sidelights and transoms on both of the rooms as well. Clients paid good money for that kind of millwork in new construction. She, Jennifer, and their grandmother had frequently daydreamed about how the house could look if someone had the money to renovate it properly. Together, they would pore over decorating magazines and clip out their favorite images of kitchens and wallpapers, window treatments and lighting. Holly had proudly informed her grandmother that when she grew up, she'd make enough money to decorate it as they had planned.

And that's exactly what she was going to do—restore this Victorian home to its former glory—and then sell it. She ignored the jolt of pain that jabbed her in the stomach, reminding her that it should have been Jennifer and Rick's house, and she should have been helping *them* plan a renovation.

Holly looked over her shoulder. Quinn was jiggling the old doorknob and fighting with the keys still stuck in the door, not paying her any attention. Even though she'd never admit it out loud, it felt good to have him here. The house was a little eerie. That was something she hadn't counted on. And she wasn't looking forward to spending the night here by herself with a baby. Heck, she didn't even feel comfortable walking through the entire house alone. Especially without electricity.

Holly jumped as she caught a glimpse of a vague shadow move across the floor. With the dim lighting, she couldn't be sure…but it was exactly the type of scurrying she would attribute to a mouse. Didn't rodents move into abandoned places? She and rodents could not co-exist. Her poor grandmother would have been mortified to think there were mice in her once-spotless home.

"Quinn?" she asked, spinning around and shifting Ella to her other hip.

"Yeah?" He looked up from the lock.

"Do you think there are mice here?"

"I don't know. Maybe. Probably," he said, shrugging, sounding infuriatingly unconcerned. Then he went back to jiggling the doorknob.

"Maybe I should pick up my bag," she thought aloud, rushing over to her purse, the wide plank floors creaking as she walked.

"Yeah, good idea. I hear Coach is the hottest fashion accessory among the mice community," he drawled.

Holly raised her brows. "I wasn't aware you were into designer accessories."

"I've been with my share of high-maintenance women, Holly," he said with a sigh, leaning against the door frame. The image of his skeletal ex-wife, Christine, popped into her mind.

"I'm not high maintenance." She frowned, not sure if she

was more upset about his reference to "being with" women, or his grouping her in with the lot of them. Especially his ex.

"Know what? You're right. You're not high maintenance," he said, and then turned back to wrestling with the keys. But not before Holly caught a look of sympathy—no, *pity*—flash across his blue eyes. Her stomach flipped repeatedly, not knowing whether that pity was due to Jennifer, or due to him remembering how she'd thrown herself at him like a slobbering, eager puppy.

"Well, thanks for helping me into the house. But I should get to work. I really need to get started on the cleaning," Holly said, lifting her chin.

"Are you kidding me? You're going to clean the house now? Tell me you're not planning on staying here tonight." Quinn had that wide-legged stance, arms folded across his broad chest, that she remembered so well, that still made her jittery with awareness. The same one she may have even seen a few times in her dreams over the last ten years. It was a far better look than the pity from a few moments ago.

Holly nodded. "That's exactly what I'm going to do." Okay, so maybe when she'd originally planned on doing this the thought of mice hadn't entered her mind, nor had the unexpected creepiness of the abandoned house. But she wasn't about to admit that to him. She was done making a fool of herself in front of Quinn.

"Why don't you stay with Claire? You two are still partners in crime, aren't you?" he asked, the corner of his mouth twitching. He was, no doubt, remembering all the trouble she and Claire had gotten into together.

"Of course we're still best friends," she said, refusing to look embarrassed. Not only were they best friends, but

Claire religiously kept her up to date on all things Red River—usually in real time. But more importantly, Claire was the best friend she could have ever asked for, and if it hadn't been for her friend's frequent trips to Toronto after Jennifer and Rick died, she didn't know how she would have gotten through the loss. "But Claire's away, and not coming home until Monday. I'm the one who jumped the gun and got here early."

Quinn frowned. "Well, how about the motel?"

"Ew. The Red River Stop and Drop?"

Quinn nodded.

"Has it had some sort of major renovation since I've last been home? Because as I recall, that dive was more of a place that people frequented on an *hourly* basis," Holly said, raising her eyebrows.

Quinn sighed roughly. "It's not that bad."

"I would need an arsenal of hand-sanitizer and anti-bacterial wipes before I set foot in that place. No thank you," Holly said, shifting Ella to her other hip for temporary relief.

"How about my house?"

"*Your* house?" Holly repeated, quickly trying to come up with a reason that would sound reasonable. She couldn't stay at his house. The last thing she wanted was for him to think she needed him—or worse, still had feelings for him.

He nodded, waiting.

"Well, I don't want Mrs. Jacobs getting wind of this and telling the entire town we've moved in together."

Quinn mumbled something under his breath. She strained to try to make it out, not knowing if he was grumbling about her or the notorious town gossip.

"It's one night."

Hard, heavy raindrops clattered against the windows, making both of them jump. It was one of Red River's infamous fall storms.

Quinn glanced outside and then back at her. "You're not staying here tonight. I'll have a team come over here first thing Monday morning and get this place cleaned up for you. We'll check for pests and all that, too, okay?"

"No thanks, we'll be fine," Holly said, forcing what she hoped was a serene expression on her face and standing a little straighter. She could handle one night here. She had no choice, really, at this point. Quinn remembered her as a lovesick adolescent. She was a grown woman now. And she could handle this house.

"Pardon?" he asked with a calm that contradicted the stiffness in his body.

"I said, we'll be fine. I can clean this place up in no time," she answered firmly, trying not to show her arms were about to spasm after holding Ella so long. She looked at the ground again. She needed to wash the floors—*after* looking for signs of mice.

"Fine. So you'd be just fine if I took off right now and left you two here alone?" he asked, glaring at her. His gruffness didn't faze her; she knew Quinn was all bluster. The sound of lightning crashing nearby made her jump, and Ella wrapped her arms around Holly's neck tightly. She heard Quinn mutter something under his breath again. The lights still hadn't turned on, and the house was darkening.

Holly nodded. "Yup. No problem."

His eyes darted from Ella to her. "Where is the baby going to sleep?"

"I have a crib for her," Holly said defensively.

"I don't see a crib." The sky illuminated behind Quinn like the Fourth of July.

"It's in the car," she replied, her eyes glancing to her SUV that was being hammered by enormous raindrops.

Quinn frowned. "You mean, in that giant box I saw?"

Holly nodded stiffly.

He raised his eyebrows. "*You* know how to assemble a crib?"

Holly's eyes narrowed. "Why do you say it like the rest of the world would know how to assemble a crib, but certainly not *I*, Holly Carrington?"

He gave her a look that told her he wasn't about to answer that. "Do you have any tools?" His tone was beginning to sound a little patronizing.

"It comes with one of those thingies, Quinn," she said, rolling her eyes and wishing she could remember the name.

The muscles in his jaw twitched as he stared at her. "A thingy?"

"You know, those L-shaped things. Really, I know what I'm doing," she said, lying through her teeth and shifting Ella to her other hip. Assembling furniture from scratch had never been her forte, but she wasn't about to admit that.

"You mean an *Allen key*?"

Holly shrugged, and Ella giggled with the motion. "Whatever, it really doesn't matter what it's called as long as I know how to use it. I'm a big girl now, Quinn. I've lived in the big bad city all by myself for ten years. I think I can handle assembling a crib and cleaning up an old house, okay?" Holly stood a little straighter, even though her back protested.

"Give me your keys. I'm going to get the crib, bring it in here, and assemble it," he said slowly, enunciating every syllable. Holly frowned at his tone. She was about to open her mouth when he held open his hand, palm side up. Ella slapped his outstretched hand and his expression changed, all the tension leaving him as he laughed with Ella and playfully slapped her hand in return. Holly watched his face transform, his eyes crinkling at the corners, his lips turning into a grin.

"Keys, Holly," he said again, giving her a brief frown before turning to make funny faces at Ella. He had some nerve.

"Quinn, there are a few words missing from your sentence. Like, *may I* and *please*."

He turned so his full attention was on her now, his face a few inches from hers, close enough that Holly had to tilt her head back slightly to meet his eyes. She didn't appreciate that. Nor did she appreciate just how perfect his face looked, even up close.

"I'm not leaving a woman and a baby in the middle of a storm in a house with no electricity and nowhere to sleep. I wouldn't do it to a stranger, and there's no way in hell I'm going to do it to you, of all people. So give me your keys."

Maybe it was the way *you of all people* sounded like a soft caress, or maybe it was just the man himself. Or maybe it was the fact that Quinn was the only man who'd given a damn about what happened to her in a long time.

Holly lifted her chin. Whatever it was, she couldn't get sucked into this. And she didn't want to get used to relying on anyone but herself. "Fine, Quinn. Thank you for your help. I'll *accept* your help. Even though I'm fully capable—"

Quinn grabbed her keys and stalked outside, the screen door bouncing against the frame as he stepped into the rain, not stopping to hear the rest of her statement.

Chapter Two

"Two country breakfasts, eggs over easy, brown toast, and two coffees, John," Quinn said in a single breath, pulling a twenty dollar bill out of his wallet.

"No prob, be out in a minute, Quinn," John said from behind the register, handing Quinn his change a moment later. John and his wife owned the country diner in downtown Red River. It hadn't been remodeled since it was first established in the fifties, but it was clean and the food was usually simple but good. It had become a kind of landmark in the town.

Quinn weaved his way past the tables of chattering people, walking to an empty booth near the window. He was preoccupied with his own thoughts as he sank into one of the vinyl, orange booths beside the window. He glanced down at his watch. His younger brother, Jake, should be here any minute. Though they worked together day in and day out in the family business, they spent a lot of their spare time together, too. And both of them knew Monday morning breakfast at John's was their "thing." Their youngest brother, Evan, was an ER surgeon in the city, and they rarely saw him during the week.

Despite his better judgment, Quinn allowed himself to reflect on his reunion with Holly on Saturday. He stared out the window as the rain poured down, giant raindrops forming endless rings in the puddles. But all he saw was Holly. He ran a frustrated hand through his damp hair. She had lived up to the promise she had shown at eighteen. No, she had surpassed it, by far.

She was cute and witty and smart at eighteen. At twenty-eight, she was gorgeous, sharp, and…wounded. He had seen Holly exactly twice in the last ten years, and both times it had been for a funeral. As much as she'd tried to hide her pain, he saw it in every expression on her face, heard it in every syllable in her voice. She was no longer the carefree girl he remembered, the girl that had offered him her heart. And then there was Ella. He knew about the tragedy with Jennifer and her husband, and that Holly was now Ella's guardian. But what he hadn't counted on was how he would react to Ella. Or seeing Holly and Ella together. Hell, he admired Holly for stepping up and rearranging her life for her niece. He didn't know what he'd do if he lost either of his brothers, let alone having to become a parent at the same time. She was brave, and she had as much guts as anyone he'd ever met. Not for one second had she let on that she was scared of anything. *Except the mice*, he thought, smiling slightly.

But his smile faded quickly. A part of him wished he could be that same man he'd been when she'd left ten years ago, before either of them had been hit with loss. He wished he could offer her what she needed. Because the first thing he'd wanted to do when he saw her was kiss her. Kiss her and taste her, and see if the reality of Holly was better than the fantasy. *That* need hadn't diminished. Even with mashed banana across his face, the only thing he'd felt like doing when she approached him with those wipes was tugging her into his body and kissing her. Exactly what he would have done ten years ago, if she hadn't been so young.

"Man, it's pouring out there!" Jake said, shrugging out of his navy raincoat with their company logo branded across the back and sliding into the booth across from him. Quinn pushed his thoughts aside and tried to look nonchalant. The last thing he wanted to do was discuss Holly, babies, or feelings with Jake.

"Yup, supposed to rain all week," Quinn said, frowning as a slow, irritating grin emerged on his brother's face.

"You've seen Holly already, haven't you?"

Quinn leaned back in the booth with a sigh. "How did you guess?"

"You look horrible," Jake said with an unabashedly amused laugh.

Quinn ran both hands through his hair, glancing over at the bar, wishing the coffee would arrive. Jake knew a little too much about his feelings for Holly. His brother knew everything that had happened—and everything that hadn't. And Jake had been the one who told him to go after Holly when she left for college. But Quinn hadn't listened. Instead, he'd let Holly go her own way, and he'd gone another. And now they were both back here, alone.

"So, how did it feel seeing her again?"

Quinn blinked, staring at his brother, looking for a hint

of teasing. He saw none. "What kind of question is that?"

"What?" Jake asked, shrugging his shoulders.

"It's a bit on the feminine side, don't you think?"

Jake scoffed. "Look, buddy, if you wanted feminine con-versation, I'd ask you what she was wearing, if she'd had any work done, and if she's gained any weight since you last saw her."

Quinn gave a snort of agreement. "Okay. Fine. Yeah, she looks pretty damn good, in case you're wondering."

"Yeah, I *was* wondering, actually."

Quinn leaned forward. "Well, you don't need to."

"Don't need to what?" Jake asked, his lips twitching slightly.

"Don't need to wonder."

Jake grinned and held up his hands. "Hey, no need to go getting all riled up, Quinn. She's all yours, buddy—the last thing I need in my life right now is a high-strung woman."

"She is high strung, isn't she?" Quinn mumbled under his breath.

"Yeah, that's putting it mildly. Did you read the scope of the project report she sent over yesterday? She made notes on her own notes. You're in for it," Jake said, glancing up as their food arrived.

Two chipped plates filled with runny eggs and greasy strips of half-cooked bacon slid across the linoleum-topped table, along with cups of coffee that swooshed over the rim.

"What the hell?" Jake muttered, looking down at the plate.

"John, did you make this crap?" Quinn called after the hastily retreating figure.

"Yeah, Joanne got pissed off and told me to do the

cooking," John yelled across the diner, his reply earning a few snorts of laughter from the other patrons. "Look, sorry, fellas, lots of problems this morning."

"*That* is why I'm never getting married," Jake quipped, as John's heavy figure scurried around the busy diner.

"Yeah, you're a smart man. Look, I'm going to be at Holly's today if you need to reach me. Got a full day lined up," Quinn said, pushing aside the plate with a shudder after trying the runny eggs.

"According to that list, you might as well clear your schedule for the next two months," Jake said, and then gagged as he tried the eggs.

"Yeah, it's a hell of a reno to get done in eight weeks," he replied. Over the years, Quinn had expanded the family business beyond renovations. In fact, they rarely did home renovations anymore. But he'd never turn down the opportunity to help Holly.

"This should be interesting," Jake said with a smirk and shoved the offensive plate of food away.

"Interesting isn't exactly the word I'd use," Quinn said under his breath.

"You haven't spoken to her in how long?" Jake asked, sipping his coffee.

Quinn scowled at his brother for a moment before answering. He couldn't remember the last time Jake had asked him so many questions that weren't work-related. "Years. Doesn't feel like it, though. But it doesn't matter, anyway," Quinn added quickly, looking out the window again. He scowled so Jake would stop talking.

"Why not?"

"Because I'm not interested," Quinn answered in the

most surly voice he could muster.

"Yeah, right."

Quinn glared at him.

"Why aren't you interested?"

"You know why."

"No, I don't. I know you've had a crappy few years. And I know Holly's been through a lot. So maybe—"

"Maybe you should mind you own business, Jake," Quinn growled. He clenched his jaw and broke Jake's heavy gaze.

"Maybe you should stop being so defensive. Maybe it's time you moved on with your life, man," Jake said.

"I have moved on. That doesn't mean I need to get married or have a kid. I like being single. What about you? You're not married."

"I'm not getting married until I'm at least forty-five. No need to ruin the best years of my life with a wife and kids."

Quinn took a deep breath and reminded himself never to enter this type of discussion with Jake again.

"Besides," Jake said with a wide grin, "you're the one who's old."

Quinn cursed at him, and then smiled in spite of himself as Jake laughed. He could never stay mad at either of his brothers. Jake had issues, but he'd changed, and Quinn knew he could always count on him. He knew both his brothers had his back. They'd been there for him when it had mattered most.

"Now, now, Quinn Manning, your mama would not have approved of that cussing." The overly shrill voice, combined with the utter boldness of the intrusion, could only belong to one person: Mrs. Eunice Jacobs, Red River's longtime town gossip.

"Oh, I know, Mrs. Jacobs. I keep telling my brother over here to watch that foul mouth of his." Jake shook his head in mock disapproval, ignoring Quinn's glower.

Quinn looked toward the offensive voice and tried to conceal his shock at the woman's bright purple raincoat with giant floating pineapples printed all over it. The vivid colors in her coat, combined with the nauseating breakfast and Jake's inquisition, made him want to hurl.

"Sorry if I offended you, Mrs. Jacobs. I didn't realize someone was standing so close, listening to our *private* conversation." Quinn softened the reprimand by giving the plump elderly woman a wide smile. He needed to get the hell out of here—fast.

"Oh, that's all right, dear. I know you're a nice boy. You should just remember to go to church more often, sweetie." She patted his hand and smiled, her bright red lips glowing like a neon sign in her pale face.

Jake snorted into his coffee.

"I hear that Holly Carrington is back in town." *So that was it.*

Jake leaned back in his seat while a massive grin spread across his face. He was obviously taking way too much pleasure from the exchange.

"Yes, she is," Quinn replied in a guarded voice.

Mrs. Jacobs swooped down close to him at the table, her owlish eyes peering into his. Quinn fought the urge to cover his face with his hands and hide under the table.

"Is she back for good?"

He took a sip of coffee, trying his absolute hardest to be polite. "Appears that way."

"She was such a sweet girl," Mrs. Jacobs said, still in his personal space. Quinn pressed himself further into the booth.

"Still is." *Damn it.*

"Really? And she always was a looker."

"That's what I was just telling him, Mrs. Jacobs," his brother said, nodding vehemently.

Quinn kicked Jake under the table. Hard. He wished he'd been wearing his steel-toed construction boots.

"You know," Mrs. Jacobs continued, absolutely oblivious to the tension at the table, "she might not mind that you're divorced. It's nothing to be too ashamed of in this day and age, Quinn. And after what happened to poor Jennifer… You know, it takes quite a woman to step up and raise a child by herself. Especially a child that's not her own. I think it's time you started looking for happiness again. You always were such a nice boy," she said with a sigh, patting him on the shoulder.

Quinn inhaled slowly and tried counting to ten.

His brother finally had pity on him, it seemed. "Mrs. Jacobs, isn't that your sister walking in?" The elderly woman snapped her head in the direction of the door.

"Oh, it is. I'll see you later, boys!"

Quinn watched the woman bustle over to her sister. "Thanks," Quinn said with a shudder. "Who knows how long that conversation could have run."

"Yeah, well, no one deserves that—especially on a Monday morning. But now, old Eunice did raise an interesting point. Did you tell Holly about Christine?"

"She knows I was married. And I'm sure she knows I'm divorced." Quinn slammed down his cup a little too hard and the black coffee splashed onto the table.

"But you didn't actually *talk* about it."

"Why would I? Seriously, your questions are irritating as hell. Are you watching daytime TV or something?"

Jake ignored him. "So where is Holly staying?"

"At the house." Quinn braced his arms wide on the edge of the table. How hard was it to have a peaceful breakfast?

"The whole weekend?" Jake nodded his head.

"Yeah. Would not leave," he said with a frown as he remembered her adamant refusal to spend the night somewhere else. It was the most difficult thing he'd done in a long time, driving away from her and the baby in that empty house with a storm raging. She was a hell of a lot more stubborn than he remembered. The power had come on shortly after he'd finished assembling the crib—the one that had needed a wrench and a power drill, which luckily he'd had in his truck. He'd gone around testing the appliances, the water in the kitchen and bathrooms, ensuring that everything was in working order. And then he'd left.

Jake shook his head and made a *tsk*ing sound.

"I don't have time for this crap," Quinn said under his breath as he rose to leave. "And I would think for someone who's dropped their pants as many times as you, you'd know a little more about women. You don't 'let' them do things. Not Holly, anyway. Like anyone has a choice with that woman. Besides, what Holly does with her life is not my business. And I'm not looking to make it my business," he growled.

"Right," Jake said with a nod and a grin.

"I'm not going to say it again, Jake," Quinn said, trying to convince himself as well as his brother. "The last thing I need is a woman in my life—especially one with a baby. So

drop it."

For a second, Quinn saw a flash of pity fire across his brother's face. But Jake knew him, and he knew the last thing he'd accept was anyone's pity.

"Holly's not just any woman."

"Seriously, Jake. I don't want a woman in my life. Besides, all of that was a long time ago. She was young and had no idea what she wanted."

"No, I think she was pretty clear that she wanted you."

He never should have told Jake anything about Holly. Quinn turned his head away, thinking back to Holly's last night in Red River. She'd been naïve and trusting—and told him that she loved him. He knew, looking into her eyes, that he loved her, too, but never said the words aloud. He didn't want to be the guy to hold her back. She'd been too young to know what she wanted for the rest of her life.

Jake's waving hand in front of his eyes jerked him back to their conversation. Quinn cleared his throat and focused. "Holly needed to go away to school, Jake. I wasn't going to make her stay here and miss that opportunity. She was eighteen—no one knows what they want at eighteen. Yeah, so she's back—but she's built a life for herself now that doesn't include me. And I don't want a baby. I *don't,*" he said with a low voice, bending down closer to the table. He didn't deserve a baby. But he couldn't admit that aloud to his brother. He knew Jake would just try to convince him that it was stupid to think that way. There was a reason men didn't talk about their feelings with each other. It was damn awkward.

"Quinn?" Jake asked, taking a sip of his coffee.

Quinn sighed. "Yeah?"

"Ten bucks says Holly will have you eatin' out of her

hands in twenty-four hours," he said with a smirk.

Quinn wished he could punch him. Instead, he stalked off, his brother's chuckle following him out the door. He didn't bother zipping up his raincoat; the rain suited his mood.

He stopped on the sidewalk outside the diner and glanced down at his watch: seven thirty in the morning. Maybe he should bring coffee to Holly. He walked back into the diner, not bothering to look in Jake's direction and ignoring the fact that he heard his name and Holly's as he passed Mrs. Jacob's table of animated elderly women.

He ordered two coffees to go.

"Have a good day, buddy. Leave the ten bucks in my truck," his brother called out to him in a voice thick with laughter as Quinn reached the door with his coffees. He cursed under his breath. Sometimes he really hated living in a small town.

. . .

Holly groaned and rolled over in her sleeping bag as the forceful knocking on the front door continued. She squeezed her eyes shut. It was too painful to contemplate moving. The rain pounding against the roof and windows incessantly was a mere whisper compared to the hammering going on in her head. What a horrible weekend. She had slept for about four hours last night—four miserable hours—thanks to what seemed like a conspiracy between Ella and what sounded almost certainly like mice. Holly did not know how it was possible that Ella knew exactly when Holly was about to drift off to sleep, and then decide *that* was the moment she should wake up. And after changing her diapers, giving her a bottle, and walking her around the house, Holly had been forced to buckle her into the car seat at two o'clock in the morning and drive around Red River to get Ella to finally fall asleep. It had been four a.m. when Holly gathered the courage to move a sleeping Ella from the car seat to the crib, and then she crawled, exhausted, into her sleeping bag on the hard wooden floor beside the crib in the living room.

The knocking continued. She stretched and groaned, looking at her watch. Seven forty. Her body ached. She had been on her own with Ella for twenty-four hours and she was already failing.

A quick glance at Ella proved she was still sleeping soundly in the crib Quinn had assembled. As she'd watched Quinn put together the complicated crib, having to go out in the rain to get tools from his car, she'd been secretly relieved that he'd insisted on doing it for her. It made her think of all the times she'd watched him from her bedroom window as he'd helped her grandfather around the old house. He'd always been there for her grandparents, for her. She had thanked him—though perhaps she didn't admit that there would have been no way she could have assembled the crib without any tools…*or at all*. Holly tiptoed out of the living room and carefully shut the French doors behind her.

She had spent the entire weekend scrubbing the first floor of the house, giving the old place a cleaning her grandmother would have been proud of. But she was glad it was Monday. Monday meant she could get this show on the road, and then get back to her life in Toronto. Back home, every-thing ran smoothly—thanks to Mary. Holly had been able to keep up with her work schedule and then come home at night and spend some quality time with Ella. Claire was back in town today, and Holly was looking forward to both moral support and help with Ella.

As Holly approached the door, she saw Quinn through the sidelights. She quickly darted away from the window before he saw her. She looked down in horror at her pajamas. Skating penguins weren't exactly the kind of nightwear she wanted Quinn to see her wearing, but she hadn't expected him to be here first thing in the morning. She crossed one arm in front of her. She should have slept with a bra on. Quinn noticed everything. She quickly tried to straighten her hair. Maybe he wouldn't notice the penguins.

"Are you going to open the door, or put on lipstick?" Quinn called out impatiently through the glass.

The last thing she wanted was him thinking she was inside primping for his arrival. Holly swung the door open. *Geez.* It should be illegal for a man to look that good this early in the morning—he was all tall lines and hard muscle, combined with a face more handsome in reality than memory.

"That's a lovely way to greet someone," she said, tightening her arm around her chest while trying to ignore the old Quinn-effect. It was even harder to do at this time of the morning and without caffeine.

"Sorry, did I wake you?" he asked, the corners of his blue eyes crinkling as he winced. She wished he'd go back to being arrogant, because compassion from him was as tempting as homemade ice cream on a hot day.

"Don't worry about it," she said, waving one hand in the air and stifling a yawn.

"I brought coffee," he said, handing her a cup.

This was getting dangerous. "Thanks."

"Glad I could help," he said with a slight smile. "So, how was your weekend?"

"Wonderful," she said proudly and took a sip of the steaming coffee.

His eyes wandered over her, and everywhere they landed she felt a traitorous heat sweep over her. "Liar. I'd say you haven't slept in days."

"Gee, thanks. You always were one for compliments."

"You're as gorgeous as always, Holly. You just look tired, that's all," he said with a low chuckle.

She ignored the praise and the flash of heat that accompanied it. "I need some fresh air. And if that baby wakes up before I finish my coffee, I'm going to poke my eyeballs out with a dull fork," Holly said under her breath as she slipped on her shoes and went to stand on the porch with Quinn. She quickly grabbed the baby monitor handset so she could hear if Ella cried. It was pouring outside, but the big veranda easily kept them sheltered and dry. She looked at Quinn, who was staring at her with a barely concealed smile.

"Here, why don't you put my coat on. We wouldn't want those penguins to get wet," he said, smiling as she choked on any chance at coming up with a clever rebuttal.

"They were the only pajamas I could find," Holly lied, looking down at the bright flannel. Actually, *all* her pajamas were a variation of some sort of flannel, but he didn't need to know that.

Quinn placed the coat around her shoulders. She put her arms through the sleeves, and the warmth of his coat engulfed her like a cup of hot chocolate. She settled on the top step next to his side and stared out at the falling rain. The effect he was having on her was powerful enough without having to look directly at him. They sat together in silence, sipping their coffee and watching the rain pelt the ground. It had been a long, long time since she'd been able to just sit and watch the rain falling. And it had been even longer since she and Quinn had sat together on these steps.

Quinn's deep voice broke the silence. "So all the trades should be here soon, and then hopefully by tomorrow morning we'll have a bunch of quotes that you can look over. This place will be cleaned and ready to go by tonight, too," he said, taking a sip of coffee and turning to look at her.

"Well, half the cleaning is already done," Holly said. She frowned when Quinn cursed under his breath, looking upward.

She sat up a little straighter. "Seriously, it needed to be done."

He shook his head, and she could see the twitching in his jaw as she stared at his strong profile. "I'm not even going to bother responding to that, Holly."

"Suit yourself." Holly sniffed, looking into her cup.

"You haven't slept a wink, have you?" he asked. This time he wasn't laughing at her. In fact, he looked oddly sympathetic. Tender, even. His voice was deep and smooth, and it coursed through her body like sweet, pure honey. And his face was far too close to hers. She could see the tiny lines at the corner of his blue eyes, and she wished for a second she knew the moments that had placed them there. She made the mistake of glancing at his mouth. For a man that radiated such masculinity, his mouth was very sensual. She quickly turned away and stared out at the overgrown front lawn littered with sodden leaves.

"You're so easy to read," he said, his lips hinting at a

smile when she looked over at him.

She leaned away from him. "Really? You know what I'm thinking?" *This should be interesting. There was no way he could know.*

"Yup," he said with a short nod.

She raised an eyebrow, challenging him. "Okay. What am I thinking, then?"

"You're thinking I'm a hell of a lot better looking than you remembered," he said with a slow, cocky smile that made her burst out laughing. It reminded her of the old Quinn. The one who always teased or made her laugh. And sitting here on the veranda with him made her ache for those days. She turned her head to look at him, letting herself indulge in the fantasy that their easy conversation was still relevant to their lives today.

"Actually, I was noticing the gray hair around your temples. Are you pushing forty yet?" she asked, sitting taller, pretending to examine his head. What she didn't add was that she found the few gray hairs very attractive, adding a sense of maturity that she didn't remember when she last saw him. She knew his exact age and birth date, and he looked more physically fit than a man ten years younger.

Quinn leaned closer to her, and she could see the laughter in his eyes. Her heart was beating wildly as he smiled at her. "I'm only thirty-five."

"Oh, right. We always were in different decades, weren't we?" Holly murmured while smiling.

Quinn's deep laugh drowned out the sound of the rain. "Yes, well, aren't you going to be entering this geriatric decade soon?"

"I still have more than a year to prepare myself," she

answered, refusing to acknowledge that a part of her was elated that he knew her age. *You're so juvenile sometimes, Holly.* She needed to end this. She had to stop flirting with him. She needed to focus on the house, get the reno done, and get out of Red River.

"There, um, may actually be *mice* in the house," Holly said stiffly, changing the subject.

Quinn sighed. "I suspected as much. Don't worry, the pest control company is one of the first people on the list this morning," he said, taking a swig of coffee, but not before she noticed his grin.

"Good. Great, I mean. I can't have mice scurrying everywhere when prospective buyers are looking around," she said with a short laugh. She didn't want him to think that she was completely petrified of the hideous little creatures that scurried around without warning. Better he thought it was just a business concern. Holly looked over at Quinn when she realized he hadn't answered. His profile was stiff, his strong jaw tense.

He cleared his throat. "You're selling the house?"

"Of course. I thought you knew that." Holly felt her chest constrict.

He gave a shake of his head. "Nope. Didn't know that. So you're going to gut your grandparents' house, renovate, and then sell it?"

The revulsion and censure in his voice made her stomach churn. "Yes," she affirmed stiffly. She had to keep her temper in check.

He finally turned to look at her. "That's a little cold, don't you think?"

Holly felt her stomach drop. "Cold?"

He nodded, his features taught and unrelenting, as his eyes stayed focused on her. Judgment was stamped across his face as clearly as a stop sign. He had no way of knowing how torturous being here was. Wherever she walked in the house, she collided with ghosts of the people she loved most in the world. She stared into his blue eyes and wanted to tell him, but there were things too close to her heart, words too painful to ever voice aloud.

"So, do tell, Quinn. What should I do? Move back to this little town, with a baby, without a job, and live in a dilapidated old house?"

"Red River is a great place to raise a kid."

"If you are *employed*."

"Why even bother to renovate, then? Why don't you just sell it and spare us both the misery of having to go through a renovation together?"

Holly's mouth dropped open. "Oh, well, excuse me. I never realized I was so repulsive to be around."

"Don't go putting words in my mouth, Holly."

"I believe you're the one who said 'misery,' not me. And you know what else, Quinn? I'm not *cold*. You want to know what's cold? How about you getting married a year after I left, after I asked you to wait for me. *That's* cold," she spat out, standing, separating herself from him.

Chapter Three

Quinn had no idea how their conversation had gotten derailed so badly. Oh, actually he did know—Holly. She had twisted everything around. Now she was standing in the damn rain looking as though she was either ready to rip his head off or cry. And, God, if he made her cry he'd never forgive himself. This isn't what he'd wanted. As mad as he was, he didn't want her to cry. She thought he'd left her?

He shook his head. "I don't get you," he said, fighting the frustration and trying to sound calm as he walked into the rain to stand directly in front of her. "You were eighteen years old, Holly. You were determined to leave. What was I going to do? I was twenty-five. I didn't expect you to wait for me. I didn't expect you to come back at all. And there was no way in hell I was going to stand in the way of your dreams."

"No," she said, shaking her head wildly. "That's an excuse. I made it clear to you. I humiliated myself with some lame-ass attempt to seduce you—"

"Holly," he groaned, hating that her face was red and blotchy with embarrassment.

"No, it's true. I was this naïve eighteen-year-old that somehow thought you felt something for me, and that if I could just get you to kiss me, you wouldn't be able to deny your feelings. But you shot me down so fast, it was obvious that it was one-sided," she said, her voice catching as she turned her head from him.

"You're wrong. You are so wrong," he whispered, running his hands through his soaked hair.

"Then why did you get married a year later?"

"I don't regret getting married," he said grimly, and then wished he could have cut his tongue off, because the hurt infused her eyes. Her mouth dropped open and she backed away a step. The rain stood between them, a physical barrier. There had always been barriers between him and Holly. But he needed to explain what he meant. He looked into the green eyes that he'd imagined so many times in the last ten years and knew that she was a different woman than the one he'd known. But she was still Holly. And he didn't want to hurt her. His words came out wrong. He didn't mean to imply that he hadn't had feelings for her, or that he hadn't wished they could have been together.

The sound of screeching tires, followed by Claire Holbrook's SUV barreling up the driveway at top speed, prevented Quinn from continuing. Holly had already turned around and was walking away from him toward the driveway. Quinn felt his opportunity pass as a few vans and trucks of various trades were slowing and turning down the drive. In about ten minutes this entire place would be buzzing. There wasn't enough time to explain something that he barely understood himself. But he'd felt the impact of her pain, of the wounded expression in her eyes, right down to his gut. It hit him harder than Jake's worst punch.

Jake was right. Back for barely a few days, and Holly Carrington was already getting to him.

. . .

"So, I see Quinn is here bright and early," Claire whispered with a smug smile as Holly closed the front door.

Holly frowned. Of course Claire would be searching for something that wasn't there. His lack of feelings toward her had made it perfectly clear they didn't stand a chance. *Cold.* That was nice. She was doing the best she could. Four months ago she'd been a basket case. She had barely gotten her life back on track, and now she was being judged by the one man who still meant something to her. Which was another issue altogether. Quinn should be just another guy. A childhood crush. Okay, fine, a teenage crush. That was it. Except for the fact that he evoked even more feelings than he had when she was younger. Including anger. That was one she'd never felt toward him when she lived in Red River. She'd first felt it when she learned that he'd gotten married. But she had gotten over that. But now, seeing him judge her made her want to yell at him. And, of course, he had practically just admitted that he still had feelings for his ex-wife. Well, wonderful.

"Why do you look like you're plotting to kill someone?" Claire asked with a worried frown.

Holly blinked a few times, trying to focus. "What? No, no, I'm just tired. And I really should go change before all

the trades come barging in," Holly said, hoping to stop that line of questioning.

Claire's eyes narrowed, but she didn't say anything more as she took off her raincoat, gently laying it on the chair beside the door. Claire was plotting. Or thinking. Or ready to intervene. "That's a nice jacket you're wearing," Claire said, her eyes narrowing into slits as they focused on Quinn's jacket.

Holly resisted the urge to roll her eyes. She wasn't about to give her any ammunition. "It's *raining*. He gave me his coat to wear. Big deal. You know what Quinn's like."

"Yes. And so do you. He's just eating up this whole damsel in distress thing like a freshly baked apple pie."

"Okay, stop right there," Holly began, holding up her hand. "First, I'm not in distress. Really. I know what I'm doing. I have a good job. I have a life. This isn't some cheesy soap opera. I'm not in trouble. And I have no interest in being rescued by Quinn or anyone else. What I'm doing, I'm doing on my own. I have a baby to raise and a career to try to maintain. And just for the record, you're wrong about Quinn. He'd run the other way."

"*Wrong!* Quinn is not a man who runs." Claire peered out the window. "Well, actually he does run. I've seen him jogging through town, and let me tell you, that is one hot body." She turned and wiggled her eyebrows, smiling at Holly.

Holly covered her ears. Claire was even more stubborn than her. "Not listening."

"Fine." Claire crossed her arms and glared at her.

Holly held up both her hands in Claire's direction, wiggling her fingers. "I'm here for eight weeks. *Eight*. That's it.

Not long enough for you to dream up some crazy reunion of a pathetic little love story that never happened. So," she said, taking a deep breath, "once again, Quinn is here for one reason and one reason only: the renovation."

"Right," Claire said, giving her a salute. "The renovation. I'm not going to say another word. Especially not about Quinn, or about all the reasons I think you should move back here. Nope, not one word." Her friend nodded, pursing her lips.

Claire never gave up that easily. Holly eyed her suspiciously. "Good. Thank you."

"Of course," Claire said, walking over and giving her a big hug. "I'm so happy you're back, even if it's just for a bit."

Holly returned the hug, relieved that conversation was over. Then Claire's nose dug into her shoulder. Holly pulled back as Claire inhaled deeply and sighed.

Holly scowled at her friend. "What on earth are you doing?"

Claire smiled. "Quinn's coat smells wonderful."

"Claire! I don't care what his coat smells like. In fact, he could smell like Pepe le Pew and it wouldn't matter. I'm not looking, or smelling, and Quinn's not interested. He thinks I'm this cold, evil woman who just wants to flip this house and take off."

"Why would he think that? There's absolutely nothing wrong with taking the house that your grandparents worked themselves to the bone to keep, that they raised you in, renovate, and then flip it. What could possibly be wrong with that?" Claire asked, tossing her hair over her shoulder. Holly wondered if someone evil had invaded her best friend's body.

"No. No way. Don't you do this to me, too. I can't move back here. You, of all people, should know that. This was not supposed to be my house. And every day that I spend here, I will be reminded of that, of what happened. I can't. It's not an option. And besides, what would I do here? How would I support myself and Ella? I have a job—a career in Toronto—a career that I gave up almost a decade of my life to pursue. I can't pack it up and move back. I have bills to pay. Do you know how much it costs to raise a baby these days? I need to sell this place. I need closure."

"Hey, hey, relax. You're not under attack. I'm sorry, I just… I want you to stay," Claire said, tears filling her eyes. "I've missed you, and I think you need us," she added, moving forward and giving Holly a hug. Holly felt her anger dissipate as she hugged her friend back, fighting her own tears.

Babbling and cooing noises interrupted them, and they both turned in the direction of the living room. Holly knew they had just a few minutes before those adorable sounds turned into ferocious crying.

"She's awake?" Claire asked, clapping her hands. "I bet she's grown, hasn't she?"

Holly smiled and shook her head. "You saw her three weeks ago. Though, I do think she's gotten even cuter," Holly said, taking her friend's hand and tugging her toward the living room.

"You know I've been training her to say Auntie Claire," Claire said with a smug grin. "And now that I'll be able to see her every day, I'm sure she'll be calling my name in no time!"

Holly's smile faltered. "Seeing you every day is going to be so great. I can't do this without you. But I'm serious.

We're not staying, okay? I need you to help me. But I can't come back here for good."

"Enough said! You go get dressed, I'll get Ella. Everything will go so smoothly, and you'll soon be wishing that you never had to leave Red River!" Claire said, shoving Holly down the hallway.

Holly was counting down the days until she could leave Red River.

Today had been a lesson in faking it. Quinn had been by her side almost the entire time—and not one personal word had been shared between them. His remark about having no regrets about getting married to Christine played in her mind like a sad, pathetic reminder that she'd meant nothing to him. And his expression had been one of regret, which had only infuriated her more, because she knew he pitied her. She needed distance between herself and Quinn, and was thankful that Claire had reined in her meddling as much as possible and taken control over Ella's needs for the day, which had enabled Holly to make lightning-fast decisions.

It was now seven o'clock in the evening, and Ella was bathed and tucked into bed for the night. Holly had temporary furniture in place, enough that she and Ella would be able to function for the eight weeks. The cleaning crew had, as promised, scrubbed the house from top to bottom. It was starting to feel livable. The fridge was stocked, clothes and baby paraphernalia unpacked, and wireless Internet installed. All she needed to do was wait for Quinn to give her all the quotes and she'd be ready to start hiring tradesmen.

She was expecting that would be tomorrow morning.

Now that the day was almost over, she was exhausted. No, beyond exhausted. In fact, she half-seriously wondered if she could somehow have caffeine hooked up intravenously. Being a single mom, or aunt, or whatever she was, was more challenging than she ever thought it would be. She remembered her old life: working a full twelve-hour day at the office and then coming home to her condo had never zapped her strength like this. She used to think she knew the meaning of tired. She would come home from work and put her feet up, eat a bowl of cereal for dinner, and maybe read a magazine. Or maybe she would have gone out for drinks after work with her colleagues. But this level of fatigue was beyond anything she had ever known. No one could have prepared her for this. And it made her doubt everything she was doing with Ella. Her sister would have known exactly what to do. Jennifer had spent almost every moment planning for Ella, even before she was pregnant. Holly knew that she was a sorry replacement for her sister, and she hoped to God that one day Ella wouldn't call her on her failings. Jennifer had always been able to let people close to her heart, she'd been so giving. But Holly had never been able to do that. She knew she held people at a distance. And she knew it was because she was afraid. She took a deep breath. *Just try your best, Holly. That's all you can do.*

She barely heard the soft knock on the front door, and then Quinn's deep voice rang out a greeting. *What was he doing here?*

"I'm in the kitchen, Quinn," she called out softly. The impact his rich, masculine voice had on the quiet house at night was undeniably comforting. And that was undeniably disconcerting.

"Hey," he said, walking into the kitchen, holding a pizza box.

"Hi," she said, her eyes darting from the cardboard box in his hand to his face. He had obviously gone home and showered, his dark hair still damp. But he hadn't shaved, his stubble accentuating his masculinity and his defined facial features. He was wearing a pale blue Henley with jeans that seemed to broadcast his tall, well-built body to a deafening pitch. She had been trying to avoid a conversation the entire day. Sitting down to dinner with him wasn't exactly going to help.

"I thought we could eat while we went over the quotes," he said, placing the pizza box on the farmhouse table.

"You got them already?" Holly asked, walking over to the table. Okay, she couldn't deny being impressed. There was one quote in particular that was of utmost importance.

He nodded, his expression tightening. "We've only got eight weeks, right?"

Holly crossed her arms. That again. "Not a day over."

His jaw clenched. "Great. Well, I hope this dinner doesn't put you behind schedule."

"It's a working dinner, so I'm sure it'll be fine," Holly said with a smile as Quinn rubbed the back of his neck, looking at the ceiling. "What can I get you to drink?"

"I wouldn't mind a beer," he said.

Holly shook her head. "Sorry, I'm not much of a beer drinker. But Claire brought a few bottles of wine. Is that okay?"

Quinn nodded, pulling out a chair at the table and sitting down. Holly walked over to the antique china cabinet, which had been scrubbed and dusted, to grab her grand-mother's old wine glasses. In the freshly washed glass doors, she stared into her reflection and wanted to pitch herself through the glass to avoid having Quinn see her like this. She felt a slow, burning sweat, and quickly turned around to look at Quinn, who was silently flipping through the folder of quotes, paying her no attention whatsoever.

"You know, I was just about to hop into the shower before you came in. Do you mind if I go now?" she asked, already tearing across the kitchen without waiting for his reply. "Help yourself to the wine in the fridge and go ahead and start eating," she called out from the hallway.

Holly stopped at the top of the stairs, listening as Quinn moved around the kitchen. She crept across the hallway to the main washroom and looked in horror at her reflection in the mirror. The formula-stained, bathwater-wet sweatshirt hung from her body like some blob that just emerged from the swamp. Her hair matted on her head like a pile of wet hay. And she looked like she hadn't slept in weeks. *Think fast, Holly.* She turned on the shower. The sexiest man she'd ever known was waiting for her downstairs, looking unbe-lievable, while she looked like something…never mind. She showered in record time, then rummaged through her over-night bag. She found a pair of jeans, undergarments, and a pink T-shirt. Oh, well, it'd have to do. Exactly seven minutes later she was running a comb through her wet hair while frantically brushing her teeth.

She looked in the mirror. Not great, but better than the pre-shower version of herself. She pulled at her T-shirt slightly, trying to loosen it. The image of Quinn's ex-wife, who looked as though she only ate on holidays, popped into her head. According to Claire, Christine hadn't aged or gained an ounce in ten years. Not that it should matter to Holly at all. *What was it that she and Claire had nicknamed Quinn's girlfriends?* She closed her eyes and then snapped them open. What did it matter anyway? After another tug at her T-shirt, she opened the door and walked down the stairs to the kitchen.

· · ·

Holly's approaching footsteps forced Quinn to focus. He had to explain what he'd said this morning about not having regrets. He felt like a jerk. Somehow he was going to have to tell her without giving her all the details. He didn't want to talk about his marriage to Christine. And there was no reason to, anyway, since Holly would be leaving.

Holly whizzed into the room and he sucked in a breath. Her damp hair tumbled around her shoulders in soft waves and smelled citrusy and fresh. Her high cheekbones were a pretty shade of pink, yet he noticed she wasn't wearing any makeup. *How could a woman look that good without makeup?* Christine had even worn makeup to bed. He could still picture her pillowcase with the leftover markings of smudged mascara, foundation, and red lipstick—it was like sharing a bed with Bozo the clown. Holly being even more gorgeous than ten years ago was something he was going to have to get used to.

"Sorry I took so long, I just really needed a shower after today." She sighed and sunk into the chair across the table from him. While she was upstairs, he'd gone ahead and opened the wine and poured them each a glass. He had a

feeling he'd be needing a hell of a lot of alcohol if he was going to discuss Christine, renovations, and prices with Holly.

"Thanks for the pizza," she said, tucking a strand of damp hair behind her ear.

"No problem. Here. I hope you like pepperoni," he said, placing two slices on her plate. He noticed she avoided eye contact. He hated the tension between them.

"Yum," she said, licking her lips. He paused, his slice of pizza halfway to his mouth. His reaction to her lip-licking was immediate and totally unexpected. *Focus. Tell her what you meant this morning.*

Holly reached for the file. "Can I have a look at the quotes?"

Quinn nodded, forcing himself not to look below her chin as he slid the folder over. Maybe he'd hold off a few more minutes before he told her.

Holly took a deep breath before opening the folder. She flipped through the pages but didn't stop to study any particular estimate. "These aren't all the quotes," she said a moment later, her brows knit together as she glanced from the papers to him.

"What's missing?" Quinn asked, reaching for the folder. He was sure everyone had bid today. He had made it clear that this was a fast, bang-it-out reno.

"The, um"—she gave a little cough—"the pest control company," she said, quickly taking a gulp of wine.

Oh, so that was it. Quinn tried not to smile. "Well, I spoke with them," he said, trying to figure out if she was deathly afraid of mice, or if it was just your garden-variety female aversion to mice.

"And?" Her hand tightened on the wine glass and she

leaned forward, perched on the end of her chair precariously. *Not* garden-variety fear.

Quinn hated lying. But there were times in life that lying to spare the people you cared about was the only option. Maybe he'd just tell her half of the truth. And then, if it looked like she could handle the rest, he'd tell her everything. "So, they uh, found some evidence of mice—"

Holly's dramatic intake of breath could have probably been strong enough to suck in the contents of what was on the table. Her face went white and she chugged down the remains of her wine, which was practically the full glass.

She leaned forward. "What does that mean exactly?"

Quinn reached over and picked up the wine bottle. He raised his eyebrows and she nodded. He quickly refilled her glass while searching for the right way to tell her the attic was a thriving mice metropolis.

"It means that they're going to put out some traps—"

"Traps? As in, Tom and Jerry traps?"

Quinn bit back his grin. He really tried his damnedest not to laugh as he stared into her wide eyes. "No, I think they're a little different."

"Are there going to be dead mice lying around?"

Quinn shook his head. "You're not going to notice anything," he said, opening the pizza box for another slice. He looked at her plate; she had taken maybe three bites. "I thought you were hungry."

She shoved her plate away. "Well, that was before I found out that mice are crawling around the house!"

Maybe now was the perfect time to talk about his ex-wife. "I wanted to explain what I meant this morning," Quinn said, clearing his throat.

Holly put her wine glass back on the table with a thud, the liquid swirling close to the rim. "You mean, when you said you were still in love with Christine?"

Quinn frowned. "I never said—"

"You said you had no regrets."

"There's a big difference between not having regrets and I'm in love with Christine," Quinn bit out, trying to keep calm. He took a long drink of his wine and then looked at her. She crossed her arms and raised her eyebrows, clearly not buying a word of it.

A loud, high-pitched cry nearly made him jump out of his chair.

"I'll be right back," Holly said with a sigh, already on her way out of the kitchen. Quinn followed without thinking. He stood in the bedroom doorway as Holly walked to the crib.

"Hey, Ella-Bella," Holly whispered in the softest, sweetest voice he'd ever heard. Ella stopped crying the minute Holly picked her up.

Quinn couldn't move, consumed by an invisible mountain of memories that made it impossible to breathe. The sweet, fresh smell of the baby's room, the soft glow of the pink ballerina night-light, and the white crib carried him back to a place he thought of daily—and one that taunted him at night.

Holly snuggled Ella against her chest, patting her back in a slow, circular motion.

"I think she might be getting a new tooth," Holly whispered, walking around the room.

As Holly turned, Ella's eyes locked onto his. He shouldn't have made eye contact. He shouldn't have looked into those innocent, wide, green eyes. Ella held out her arms and Quinn was held hostage on the threshold of past and present. He looked at Holly, and he could see the confusion in her face. He opened his mouth to say something, while in his head he commanded his feet to back up and get the hell out. But then Ella's face scrunched up and her eyes filled with tears as he stood there, stupidly staring, not moving.

"Quinn, I—"

Quinn walked into the room, telling himself he could do this. He felt a cold sweat break out as he opened his arms and settled Ella against his chest. When her head instinctively cuddled into the nook between his neck and shoulder, her soft, fluffy hair tickling his chin, his arms constricted. Her fuzzy pink sleeper, her precious weight, her innocence touched every part of him that he'd closed off.

Ella's fingers curled around his shirt and she cuddled into his chest. So much trust. God, as he stood there holding her, he wanted nothing more than to keep her safe. He wanted to be able to promise the world to the both of them.

He felt Ella sigh, and every part of him ached. He couldn't do this. He didn't deserve this baby that was cuddling against him. He'd lost that privilege years ago. Breathing became laborious as fear replaced the air in his lungs. He was a coward. And he needed to get the hell out of here.

"Holly, I, uh, I have to go," he said, cringing at the vulnerability in his voice.

He handed Ella over, and he didn't look into either of their eyes, knowing disappointment would be stamped across them.

Get out, Quinn.

Chapter Four

Holly sat cross-legged on the uneven, wide-plank wooden floor in the attic. She was surrounded by boxes filled with mementos from her childhood. The sun streamed through the large, arched window, its light ushering in reassuring warmth. The smell of musky old books was comforting as she pulled out an old photo album. Holly rubbed her hand over the floral vinyl cover, trying to psych herself up for the onslaught of memories that opening the album would evoke.

Holly flipped through the sticky pages, pausing as she came across a picture of her mother. She had no real memory of her—she had died when Holly was only three—but photographs of her mom always brought a sense of longing and loss. She knew only what her grandparents had told her—that she'd been kind and gentle and loving. She knew where her mother had gone to school, what her favorite foods were—all the things a child would think to ask. And she knew the general details of their father, as told to her and

Jennifer by their grandparents. Not long after their mother had died, their father had left them. She often wondered if he had ever loved them at all, to just walk away from them in their time of need. But their grandparents had been the most wonderful parents they could have ever asked for, and they had raised them with so much love and care that Holly and Jennifer had never wanted for anything.

Holly took a deep breath, closed the album, and resumed her search for the stack of magazines. After a few more minutes of exploring, she found the pile of old decorating magazines that she, her grandmother, and Jennifer had pored through on weekends. She held the thick folder in her hands for a moment before opening it. On the top of the stack were the cutouts of their favorite designs, held together by a pink paper clip. With a wistful smile she flipped through the pictures and let the memories come. Every Sunday night, Holly and Jennifer would sit on the rug by the fireplace, while their grandmother sat on the rocking chair beside them, and look through the magazines together. Their grandfather would sit and read his newspaper and occasionally look over at them, his green eyes twinkling at their lively discussion. Holly could still smell the rich aroma of freshly brewed coffee and just-baked cinnamon bread. Tears stung her eyes as she imagined what it would be like to be back there, with all of them, even just for a few minutes. She owed it to all of them to make their vision a reality.

She wrapped her hand around the baby monitor receiver beside her and turned up the volume until she heard the gentle sound of Ella's deep, even breathing. She held it against her ear and took a deep breath. Everything was going to be okay. Ella was fine. She was *fine*. They would live a long life together and they'd be happy. Despite professing this to herself on a regular basis, more often than not she would lie awake in bed while her mind wandered to all the what-ifs. All the things that could go wrong. All the reasons why she was not the right person to raise Ella. In Toronto, getting a nanny for Ella had been the obvious solution. But the past two weeks here in Red River, her thoughts of some-how managing a career and seeing more of Ella were tempting. But that line of thinking was dangerous. It terrified her. Loving Ella was easy. But admitting that she loved her like a mother would love a daughter filled her with such terror and guilt that she promptly shoved aside those thoughts. She was not Ella's mother. She would never be a good enough re-placement for Jennifer. Slowly lowering the volume on the receiver, Ella's gentle breathing fading into the background, Holly rolled her shoulders and stretched.

She took a deep breath and looked around the attic. She took in the proportions of the large space—its sloped ceiling, the staircase, the large window—it would make the perfect home office. Except since she was selling the house, it would be pointless to do an attic reno. The cost would override the payoff. *Selling* the place. The last two weeks had been so busy that whenever guilt would trickle in, she'd been able to push it aside in order to deal with the demands of the reno-vation and Ella. She kept reminding herself that she had no choice—living here was not an option. The house, the peo-ple, were just reminders of a life that didn't exist anymore.

Seeing Quinn briefly throughout the weeks had con-firmed this. After he practically stormed out of the house after holding Ella, their encounters had been strictly profes-sional, a poignant reminder that they had never been more than friends. And evidently, he didn't want to let her in. And that was fine. Closer was not what either of them needed. They both had their own lives, their own careers, their own pasts. There was no point rehashing old issues or creating new ones.

The two weeks had passed without any major incidents. The people that Quinn had recommended for the renovation were stellar and basically ran the show flawlessly. Quinn was swamped with starting up some new project, and he was only popping into the house every day to make sure things were under control. That made things a bit easier for Holly, but curiosity about the kind of man Quinn had become had gotten the best of her, and she found herself covertly watching him interact with the trades. He had an air of authority about him and carried himself with confidence. She could see how he'd transformed the small family business into the thriving enterprise it was today.

Holly froze and her jaw dropped open as her eyes focused on a familiar, hand-sewn fabric pouch. It sat on the middle shelf of the old wooden bookcases across the room. The floor creaked as she walked across the attic, sidestepping random pieces of furniture and stacked boxes.

Her heart started beating wildly as she picked up the soft velvet pouch and held it in her hands. *No way*. She had almost forgotten about this. A rush of heat infused her face as she toyed with the satin drawstring. The words "Holly and Quinn" were hand stitched in the velvet. She stared, almost not wanting to open it. The memory of the day she and Claire had made these was so clear that it was hard to believe it had been nearly fifteen years ago. They had been seated on her white eyelet comforter in her pink bedroom, with piles of magazines and cans of Diet Coke surrounding them. They had propped her desk chair under the doorknob to make sure no one barged in on them while they were working on their sewing.

Holly looped her finger through the satin tie and tiptoed over to the stairwell, confirming that the door to the attic was closed. She needed absolute privacy opening up this pile of embarrassing teen artifacts. Fortunately, Quinn was away for the day at a business meeting, so she knew she didn't have to worry about him walking in on her. Once privacy was secured, she scurried over to sit on an old milk crate in front of the window. She couldn't stop the smile that found its way to her lips as she pulled open the drawstring and dumped the contents of the bag onto her lap. A picture of Quinn, who must have been in his early twenties, landed on the top of the pile. She almost groaned out loud as she riffled through the stack of mementos. She found Christmas cards and birthday cards that he had sent to the family. She had kept everything remotely related to Quinn. She stopped for a second when she spotted a magazine clipping of a wedding dress. She would have burst out laughing, except for the fact that she was the orchestrator behind the ridiculous item. She fumbled around and took out her cell phone—Claire really needed to be reminded of this. There was no reason she had to be subjected to this embarrassment by herself. It was a nice feeling, knowing that her best friend was a part of her daily routine again. Claire was just a five-minute drive away, and there hadn't been a day she hadn't seen her since she and Ella had been in Red River. She refused to think about how she was going to get along without Claire when she was back in Toronto. Holly held the phone to her ear, waiting for

Claire to answer, while she continued poring through the contents devoted to all-things-Quinn.

"Claire's Flowers." Claire's chipper voice answered on the third ring.

Holly swallowed the laughter that was dying to break free from her chest. "Claire, oh my God, are you sitting down?"

Claire inhaled sharply. "Why? What's wrong?"

Holly took a deep breath. "You have no idea what I've just found. Something so mortifying, you've probably repressed the memory, something—"

"Holly, I thought this was an emergency."

"Oh, this is an emergency all right. If you only knew what—"

"Spill."

Holly swallowed a large gulp of air, not ready to relinquish this secret yet. It felt so good to actually laugh. And be silly and childish. "This is big, Claire. Think. Something so embarrassing that it would make us both look like crazy teenage stalkers."

"This is cruel," Claire hissed into the phone. Holly almost fell off the milk crate as she found a picture of her and Quinn in front of her grandparents' Christmas tree. Quinn's arm was around her in a purely platonic gesture, and she was standing beside him, her braces glistening under the glow of the Christmas tree lights as she smiled up at him adoringly. She was wearing the T-shirt that he had given her for Christmas. On the front was the word "Dream" in glittering pink. Oh, that T-shirt! She had worn it so many times.

"Claire, just think. C'mon."

"Our old binoculars?" her friend whispered, her voice

oozing with embarrassment.

Holly stifled her laughter. "Nope. Way worse."

"The movie stubs from when we followed Jake and Quinn into the theater?" Claire asked in a low, stilted voice.

Holly wiped the moisture from her eyes as she laughed at the memory. She had almost forgotten that one. "Keep guessing." Her eyes quickly surveyed the room. That shirt had to be up here somewhere. She darted across the attic to the section with the clothes boxes. She couldn't remember the last time she'd felt so free. Holly spotted the box labeled "Holly's High School Stuff." She unfolded the lid, and half-way down, underneath the dated clothing, was the prized shirt. "Hold on, Claire," she said, placing the phone on a closed box. Without giving it a second thought, she threw off her sweater and pulled on the shirt. *Ouch.* How skinny had she been? She had worn that T-shirt over and over again. It was practically threadbare. She ran her index finger over the faded words, and for the briefest of moments felt a connection with the girl she was back then. She picked up the phone, anxious to resume their conversation.

"Hi, sorry, I'm back. I just found the T-shirt that Quinn gave me for Christmas when I was fourteen."

"Uh, that's really great, Holly, but I've got a store full of customers," Claire whispered.

"Okay, okay. I'm warning you though, you should sit down. I'll give you a hint: mine is red and you had a blue one with the words Jake and Claire embroidered on the front." Holly had tears running down her face as she heard Claire shriek on the other end of the phone as she finally clued in, and then apologized to the customers in the flower shop. She was laughing so hard with Claire that the loud footsteps bounding up the attic stairs didn't register until it was too late.

"Holly, is that you up there?" The sudden sound of Quinn's deep voice made her scream out loud. She threw the pouch, the photographs, and her phone in the air and slapped her hands over her mouth as she spun around in the direction of the stairs. She could have sworn she heard Claire yelling the words *"die"* and *"kill you"* as the phone crashed to the ground.

"Sorry, did I scare you?" Quinn was standing in front of her, looking very much unlike the Quinn she was used to. He was dressed in an exquisitely tailored navy suit that accentuated his broad shoulders and tall, lean body. His white shirt stood out against his tanned skin and dark hair, and the pale blue tie reflected the color of his eyes.

"What are you doing here?" she yelled, darting around him and frantically collecting the incriminating artifacts.

"I brought coffees," he said in a stilted, confused tone as he watched her scrambling around.

"I thought I was up here by myself," she said breathlessly. *Where was the pouch?* Her eyes surveyed the floor, quickly glancing over her cell phone, through which she heard Claire yelling her name. She should probably pick that up and tell her she'd call later.

"Is someone on the phone?" Quinn asked as his eyes shifted to her phone.

"No," Holly said, pressing the end call button, as Claire's voice raged through the earpiece. She'd deal with Claire later.

"Why are you in the attic, anyway?" he asked again, frowning at her.

"Nothing, nothing, just sorting through things," Holly said, trying to sound casual as she scanned the room for that stupid pouch.

Quinn's eyes were riveted on the back corner. The pouch couldn't have landed all the way over there, could it? "Did you notice anything strange up here?"

Uh, yeah. Evidence that I was a teen stalker. Holly shook her head and tried to plaster a serene expression on her face. "Nope. Nothing at all."

He didn't look convinced as he placed the paper coffee cups on one of the milk crates. "Nothing?"

"Nope," she said, backing up slightly as she felt the soft fabric at her feet. All she had to do was bend down and pick it up.

Quinn's face relaxed and he nodded. "Good."

"So, everything going well downstairs?" she asked, surreptitiously pushing the pouch aside with her foot. His eyes slowly went from her face to her foot. She held her breath. She smiled as sweetly as she could, trying to stand perfectly still.

"You lose something, Holly?"

Holly shook her head slowly, not breaking eye contact with him as the uncomfortable realization that he was on to her dawned.

"So, you wouldn't be looking for this?" he asked, bending down to pick up the pouch. Holly bit down on the curse that was about to fly out of her mouth. The amusement in his voice said it all. She could feel herself beginning to tremble with mortification as he straightened himself up to his towering height. And there it was, the red velvet pouch in Quinn's large, tanned hands. And Quinn was wearing an infuriatingly gorgeous smile on his face.

She looked him straight in the eye as she tried to snatch the bag from his hands.

He held on.

"Quinn, let go!" She tugged at the string.

"Wait, I want to see what this is," he insisted, his blue eyes teasing. "After all, my name is on it." Every breath she took sunk her deeper into the humiliating abyss of her Quinn-stalking years. He traced his long fingers over her inscription. She wished she could fall through the floor and crash down into the kitchen. No, further... Into the basement. Maybe then she wouldn't have to explain.

She braced herself for the teasing as he looked up at her. But Quinn's face was serious. The tenderness that she'd witnessed a few times since she'd been back flickered across his face. She decided she should speak first and try to save face. "Quinn, I'm not sure if you remember, but...but I had a little, teensy"—she made a motion demonstrating just how small with her fingers—"crush on you when I was a teenager. You know, before that last night, when I completely humiliated myself."

He looked into her eyes, the disconcerting tenderness still there. "I know. And you didn't humiliate yourself."

Holly swallowed and nodded, feeling like a total idiot. Of course he knew. At least he was being honest. On some level she knew she hadn't been that subtle back then. But it was a little disturbing that he was getting a glimpse of just how much of a "crush" she'd had. She crossed her arms over her chest.

Quinn sent her a look that she hadn't seen before. One that sent shivers up and down her spine. He took a step

closer to her, and she could smell his fresh cologne, its mas-culine scent teasing her senses.

She forced herself to smile even though she was ready to run for safety. "It was a long time ago, really, Quinn," she said, backing up farther as he took another step closer. At least he wasn't looking at the bag anymore. But then, when his eyes did a slow perusal over her body, she wondered if maybe she'd prefer him looking at the bag.

"Holly?" His voice was rich and sweet like honey.

Holly cleared her throat in an attempt to sound normal. "Yeah?"

"You kept the shirt." *The shirt!* She had forgotten about the shirt! Her face felt like it had just been lit by a blowtorch as his eyes dipped down and landed on her breasts for a few hot seconds. Everything in the room suddenly slowed, throbbed, and then pulsed ahead.

"It's uh"—she crossed her arms in front of her as she tried to appear nonchalant, despite the lack of air in her lungs—"I just found it up here and thought it would be fun to try it on…it's obviously a little small," she said, tugging at the shirt. *Just shut up. Stop talking, Holly.*

His jaw clenched and he gave her a slight nod, his eyes doing a thorough appraisal of her. "It looks a hell of a lot better than I remember."

Good grief. She stepped back and banged into the book-cases behind her, yelping as a cascade of books came tum-bling down over her.

"Are you okay?" Quinn asked as she slowly peered out from her hands.

She nodded, feeling her cheeks burning. She forced her-self to tilt her chin up and look as though nothing remotely embarrassing had happened.

"Seriously, though, what are you doing up here?" he asked, stepping a little closer to her.

"Trying to kill myself, obviously," she choked out, shaking the dust off her hair.

He smiled. His eyes sparkled and danced until they landed on her mouth. A decadent shiver ran through her body as Quinn moved within inches of her. Her mouth went dry at his proximity, at the heat that radiated from him.

"Look, Quinn. Normally I am a very put-together person. Very *graceful*, well-dressed, poised, and all of a sudden—"

He leaned down a little, the corner of his delicious mouth turned up slightly. "It's because of me."

Luckily the arrogance of that statement poured some cold water over the rising temperature of her body. She narrowed her eyes. "Pardon me?"

He straightened himself up. "I make you nervous."

"Oh, you do, do you?" She crossed her arms defensively as he looked at her all smug and confident in his suit.

"Yup," he said with a self-satisfied grin. She was irritated that Quinn looked as good in a suit as he did in his everyday work jeans. She wished he'd have looked awkward all dressed up. Instead, he'd handled it like he did everything else—with smooth, unmistakable confidence. *And arrogance, don't forget the arrogance, Holly.*

"What makes you think you make me nervous?"

"Well, your heart is racing a mile a minute, your face is all blotchy—"

"That's because I almost died under a pile of falling books!"

"Mmm-hmm." His eyes flickered down to her mouth

again. "Holly," he said in a deep, gravelly voice that made her toes curl. Her eyes flew up to his, and she licked her lips.

"Yeah?"

"I don't know if I told you, and I know things have been kind of crazy since you arrived, but it's good to have you back," he said.

She tucked a strand of messy hair behind her ear. "It's, um, good to be back."

He gave a short nod. "If you need anything, you know you can call me anytime, right?"

Holly nodded slowly. "Of course, thanks."

He cleared his throat, and for a second a look of discomfort crossed his face. "I also never got to finish explaining about Christine that night," he said.

"You don't owe me an explanation," she whispered, even though she wanted one. But she didn't want to go down that road. A logical explanation that would make them connect and take them from old friends to…

• • •

Quinn fought the urge to reach out and touch her. Standing in front of him, with her hair all messy and dusty, her cheeks flushed, she was the most appealing woman he'd ever known. Mix that with a mouth that was so damn kissable and a body that had his mind wandering to all the things he'd love to spend an afternoon doing with her, he was finding it difficult to concentrate.

So many things had been left unresolved between them, and he didn't like it. Until Holly came back, his life was black and white. Simple. He didn't do complicated—and

Holly was the epitome of complicated.

Since he'd left that night after holding Ella, he'd been tempted to drive over here and explain everything. Holly deserved the truth. As much as he hated talking about it, she deserved the truth from him. He owed her. But now he was up here flirting with her.

The memory of Holly as a teenager was achingly sweet. Her grandparents had been wonderful people. As they aged, he and his brothers would come by to help out with odd tasks here and there. Quinn had really gotten along with her grandfather. And Holly had been the apple of her grandfather's eye.

During her teen years, Holly would always find excuses to hang around him, and he'd indulged her. But when she turned seventeen, something began to change in their relationship. Their conversations had turned deeper, and he found himself enjoying her company more than he should have—he was attracted to her. An undercurrent had started. At first barely noticeable, but then, month by month, it grew in force, until Quinn had to distance himself. He was too old for her and it didn't feel right. They were seven years apart, and he was a man, and she a young girl. Now, the age difference didn't matter much. But when she was eighteen to his twenty-five, it seemed like worlds apart.

Quinn stared at Holly, unable to get the image of her on the doorstep the night before she left for school out of his mind. He remembered everything: the soft curve of her lip, the smell of her hair, of her skin. And he'd never forget the briefest taste he'd had of her. Before he'd come to his senses.

"Hey, Quinn!" A loud voice boomed from below. Jake. Quinn grit his teeth. Holly broke eye contact with him, and

A Risk Worth Taking

he backed up a few steps. Quinn sighed, his eyes leaving hers, and he walked over to the doorway slowly.

"What?" Quinn called down impatiently. Holly joined him at the top of the stairs as Jake opened the door.

"You, uh, might want to come to the en suite and see this," Jake said, his eyes darting from his to Holly's. *Crap.* He knew exactly what this was going to be about.

Quinn turned to give Holly a quick and what he hoped was a casual smile, before turning to his brother. "Sure, be down in a second," he said. Jake gave him a nod and walked away.

"I'm coming, too," Holly said in that huffy tone she used when she thought she was being excluded from a decision in the renovation. It was a tone he heard at least once a day.

His back stiffened as he paused on the last step. "No need, I've got it."

"No, I insist, especially since *I'm* the only designer here *and* the owner of the house."

He swallowed the curse at the tip of his tongue. Amazing that he could go from turned on to irritated in about two minutes.

He sighed, his hand on the doorknob as he turned around to face her. "Somehow, I don't think this is going to be a design issue." If this was what he thought it was, having Holly around was going to be a disaster.

"Doesn't matter," she said, following him down the stairs.

"Fine. You may want to change your shirt first, though," Quinn said with a grin at her infuriated expression. Perfect, that should buy him a few minutes. He walked down the stairs and almost tripped as he realized the laugh was on him, considering how good that shirt looked on her. And that just a mere few seconds ago he'd been thinking about how he'd like to peel that shirt off of her.

Quinn whipped open the door, then strode down the hallway and through the master bedroom to get to the en suite. It had been Holly's idea to add an adjoining washroom to the principal bedroom, and he had to admit it would be a major selling point for today's buyer.

"The guys took down the ceiling in here and, uh, came across this," Jake said as Quinn stood in the doorway of the gutted room. Quinn looked up and cursed loudly. Holly was going to freak if she walked in here. Maybe he could shut the door and deal with it himself.

"So what's up?" Holly called out, sounding close by. Quinn almost jumped. How the hell had she made it down here so fast? He didn't turn around, hoping that he was blocking enough of the doorway that she wouldn't be able to get in.

She poked him on the shoulder. He turned his head slowly, trying to come up with something that would make her actually listen to him.

"Nothing's up. Everything's fine and under control," he said, lying blatantly through his teeth.

Holly's eyes narrowed.

He tried to maintain eye contact and wished he were a better liar or she were less astute.

"Tell me what's going on," she said in a stern voice.

"You're toast," his brother mumbled under his breath. Quinn ignored him.

"Holly." He sighed. She tried to sidestep him, but he blocked her path. He felt like he was in the second grade

again as he crossed his arms and stood firm.

She frowned at him again. "Why are you acting like a bully?"

Quinn ignored the muffled laughs he heard coming from the guys inside the bathroom. His brother's was the loudest. He needed to get Jake to a new job site. Quinn shook his head. "I'm not. There's nothing to see. Let's go—"

"I'm not going anywhere except in there," Holly said, ducking under his arm.

"Don't look up," Quinn called out harshly.

Chapter Five

Of course, *up* was the first place she looked.

And almost lost her lunch. Everything stopped. Breath, thought, motion. And then self-preservation kicked in and she backed right out. Into the hard wall that happened to be Quinn. She could feel everyone's eyes on her.

Don't lose it, Holly. Just keep cool. Breathe. Do what a normal person would do if they walked into a room, looked up, and saw that there were at least a dozen or so dead mice trapped between the pink insulation and the clear plastic vapor barrier. She tried taking a deep breath. There just wasn't any air to breathe. And even if there was any available oxygen, it was surely contaminated by the dead-mouse air.

Holly looked up again, then squeezed her eyes shut. Then she felt Quinn's hands on her shoulders. Large, confident, strong. The exact opposite of how she felt at the moment.

"So, I see there's a little bit of a problem here?" Holly

managed to croak, opening her eyes. She thought she sound-ed pretty convincing. Except that everyone's eyes went over hers to look at Quinn. She wasn't going to turn around and let him see her face, which she was sure was extra "blotchy."

"It's a minor issue," Quinn said, his voice rough, the squeeze he gave her shoulders extremely gentle. "We've got two choices. We can leave things as is, put the ceiling back up, or we can get into the attic, rip out all of the insulation, then re-insulate."

"Yup. That. Rip everything out," Holly said, nodding frantically and waving her arms. *Like really, was there a choice?*

"Holly, these mice have been dead for years. If you're going to sell the place anyway, why don't we just put the ceil-ing back up and not deal with it? Dead mice aren't going to hurt anyone," Jake said.

"Get rid of it, Jake," Quinn said, his breath rustling against her hair.

"That means at least another few days of work—"

"Just do it." Quinn sighed.

Jake frowned and then peered up at the ceiling. "And I don't even know how much it will cost—"

"Doesn't matter. Oh, what's that noise? I think I hear my cell phone," Holly said in a high-pitched voice that hurt her own ears and ducked under Quinn's arm. She did her fastest walk short of a run from of the room and flew down the stairs.

Holly banged open the screen door with the palm of her hand and burst onto the empty front porch. Her house was filled with mice. Dirty little mice that just appeared out of nowhere. Without warning. And she had been about to lose it until she felt Quinn's hands on her. The imprint of Quinn was still on her back. It was as though she'd backed into a wall. Except the wall had been alive and breathing and hot. Comforting, electrifying, and tempting all in one. For the briefest of seconds, before pride had brought her back to reality, she had wanted to accept the comfort she felt, that she knew was being offered, as his strong hands had squeezed her shoulders.

The vibration of her phone in her pocket reminded her that she'd left Claire hanging earlier. When she pulled out her phone and glanced at the Caller ID, she noticed it wasn't Claire—it was The Martin Group. More specifically, Daniel. This was the longest she'd ever gone without thinking about her job. She hadn't thought about it in days. She hadn't thought about her clients, the projects she'd put on hold, the color in the Thorntons' front foyer. It was one o'clock in the afternoon, when she'd typically be in her office, drinking a giant latte and going over designs at her desk.

The vibration of the phone in her hand was relentless. Holly took a deep breath. "Hey stranger," she answered, trying to sound engaged.

"Hey there, Holly. How's it going?" Daniel's deep voice made her smile. Of all her colleagues, she and Daniel had clicked from the beginning. That had eventually led to them dating briefly. She leaned against the railing and looked out onto the front yard.

"Good. *Great*. I just found out the house is filled with rodents, but other than that, everything's moving ahead of schedule," she said, almost smiling as Daniel laughed on the other end of the phone.

"Well, I'm sure you'll be able to handle it. Listen, Holl, I'm calling because the Thorntons wanted to bump up the start date on their vacation property, and since you're not going to be back in time"—he coughed—"Martin asked me to take it over."

Holly's stomach churned. Wow. That was fast. She had spent countless hours with the Thorntons, getting to know them, wining and dining them, all in an effort to secure them as clients. And now…she was gone from work for barely three weeks and they were being handed to Daniel? On a rational level she knew, of course, that if they wanted to get started on a new project, Martin had to keep them happy. And yes, she hadn't thought about them in weeks, but that didn't mean that when she was back at work they wouldn't receive top priority. But still… Panic started slowly swirling. Taking a leave of absence from work had felt like the only option. Martin had been gracious in allowing her to do this, and he knew that Holly had never taken a sick day until Jennifer and Rick. But her career was still everything. And she needed that job. The sale of this house would secure Ella's future. But her salary was what they were going to live off of. And she wasn't going to throw away her career. Holly looked down at her chipped fingernails, her running shoes, jeans… Talk about a different life…

"Holly, you still there?" She could hear the worry that laced his voice. What was she supposed to say?

Holly cleared her throat. "Of course, I am. I'm totally okay with that, Daniel, good luck. They're a little on the demanding side."

"Thanks, sweets. I met with them this morning and they seemed reasonable and anxious to get started."

He had already met with them? "Great. Well, good luck."

He sighed. "Holly, you're not mad are you?"

"Mad? Why would I be mad?" she asked, trying to sound casual. No, she wasn't *mad*.

"Okay, good. Hey, we're all looking forward to your big party. Martin mentioned it this morning, so be sure to text the details, okay?"

The open house that she was planning would be a celebration and a strategic move, a great way to showcase her work on the renovation. She knew her friends would make the two-hour drive for her, and Martin would remember why he loved her designs. She'd quickly be back in their good graces.

"Sure. Good luck, Dan," Holly said, ending the call without waiting for his reply. Her eyes rested on Quinn's truck parked at the top of her driveway. And inevitably she thought of the differences between Quinn and Daniel. She knew it wasn't fair to compare, and it wasn't as if she was with either man. She had ended things with Daniel before they barely even began. And if she were honest with herself, she knew the real reason was because of the man inside her grandparents' house—the one that made her feel like if there was anyone she'd ever let in, it would be him.

• • •

Quinn raced down the stairs. Holly was going to be the death of him. Of course she had to look up. And even though he knew it was stupid, and it really was her own fault for not listening to him, he felt bad for her. He'd never admit it to her, but Holly being afraid of something was a bit of a shock. After stopping to ask someone if they'd seen her, he made his way out to the front porch. Sure enough, there she was, her back to him, staring straight ahead at the damp yard littered

with fallen leaves.

"Hey," he whispered, standing beside her, anxious to see the expression on her face.

"Hi," she said, looking up at him and then away. He noticed she was holding her phone in her hands.

"Everything okay?" he asked cautiously.

She nodded. "It was just work," she said, her voice sounding heavy. He didn't really know much about her work other than that she was an interior designer. He couldn't forget that, since she kept reminding him every time he offered his opinion on the renovation.

"They surviving without you?" he asked, imagining what Holly would be like in an office. She probably ran the damn place. And she was undoubtedly a workaholic. He liked thinking of Holly as successful and in control, fulfilling the dreams she'd left for. But the more he hung around her, the more he was beginning to see she was also an expert at denial. Seeing her hurt or scared stirred him. It made him wish he could step up and take care of her.

She crossed her arms. "The team at Martin Laurence has no problem going on without me."

"*The* Martin Laurence?"

"Yup," she said with a half smile.

He felt proud of her. Hell, if she worked for the country's top firm, she was obviously doing great. "I had no idea you worked for him."

"Yeah. I started as an intern and then worked my way up. Really it just boiled down to a lot of long days and nights working my butt off trying to impress him until he made me a senior designer." He wasn't surprised she was senior designer at her age, but it also made him wonder if the idea he'd been contemplating would be remotely interesting to her at all. Martin Laurence was an entirely different type of environment than what he was planning on offering her.

"I'm sure it's more than that. You're really young to have a position like that," he said, watching her closely. The smile that emerged on her face as she looked up at him was so damn cute and mischievous that he felt himself smiling back, without even knowing what she was going to say.

"Well, I know to *you* I must seem very young, but really, twenty-eight isn't all that young," she said, rolling back on her heels.

Quinn threw his head back and laughed, wondering how the hell she could do that to him. He loved that she laughed along. And he loved *how* she laughed. It was natural and feminine and just about as intoxicating as the woman herself. And when he looked at her again, when the laughter subsided, he wanted nothing more than to kiss her. And hold her. And take care of everything.

"So, how long till that situation is dealt with?"

Quinn pictured her in that tight T-shirt again. And then remembered the way she had fit so nicely against him upstairs, her back and the curve of her bottom fitting so sweetly against him. Really, was there an end to their situation? The only ending he saw to this was the both of them taking care of the unfulfilled desire between them. The problem with that plan was that sleeping with Holly would only bring on a thousand more complications. And then she'd leave—for good.

"Quinn?"

He looked over at her. Her eyebrows were raised and she was waiting expectantly. *Right.* "The mice?" he asked, hoping that's what she had asked about.

She nodded rapidly.

"I didn't know you were so afraid of mice."

Holly was shaking her head. "Me? No, no, I'm not afraid of mice—" she said, her hands flying to her chest, and he refused to think how his hands would be much better there. He groaned inwardly. None of this was going as planned. He had come here today, coffees in hand, to try to explain the whole Christine thing. But instead he'd gotten caught up with Holly and her crush on him and had behaved like a schoolboy flirting with her. All it had taken was her wearing a tight T-shirt and he'd lost all direction. And then there was the mouse drama. Now he was out here on the porch, still nowhere near to discussing what he originally had intended. And those coffees were sitting cold in the attic—that was infested with mice. How the hell she had missed the black-box mouse traps up there, he had no idea. Quinn yanked on his tie as he looked at her standing there all huffy. He should really leave—for the rest of the day.

"Holly, why can't you admit you're afraid of something?" he asked, trying to filter the exasperation from his voice.

She crossed her arms. "I'm not afraid of mice, okay? I just don't like how they surprise you. I mean, if there were some sort of warning before they came into the room, then fine, maybe. But the fact that they just appear when you least expect them is very disconcerting." Quinn tried to follow her train of thought.

"Why would a mouse announce himself before he walked into a room?"

She made an irritated *tsk*ing noise and frowned at him. "Never mind. Anyway, mice carry viruses. I don't *like* them," she said, lifting her chin. "And it's not healthy for Ella." He saw the pride, the defensiveness. He knew that look. And it made him feel bad. Because it reminded him of how alone she'd been this last year, and all that she'd been through. Suddenly, he didn't want to leave anymore. He didn't want to tease her about the mice. And he wasn't going to tell her that when they'd been standing in the attic, he'd seen a mouse. Nope.

Quinn nodded slowly. "Fine. Well, I've told the crew to pull out that insulation and get it all cleared out. They took off for lunch, but they'll get started on that when they get back, okay?"

She flashed him a small smile. "Great. Thanks."

The impact of her smile hit him in the gut.

Quinn noticed the receiver Holly had clipped to her jeans. "How's Ella sleeping through all this racket?" Wasn't he supposed to be leaving? Why was he asking about Ella?

"I bought one of those sound machine things that play white noise or ocean waves. I thought it would do a good job of drowning out the noise of the workers. So far, so good," she said, knocking on the wooden railing.

Quinn nodded. *Go now, buddy. You've had your answer to the pressing question of how a baby is sleeping through renovations, now you can leave.* "Good idea."

"Well, thanks for dropping by. Now that those guys are out of the en suite, I want to get in the master bedroom and hang the chandelier that arrived yesterday."

Quinn clenched his teeth and stifled the groan of aggravation that was threatening. She was going to hang a chandelier? So much for leaving.

· · ·

Holly was surprised Quinn was still here. He was standing close enough to smell his cologne and see the pulse beating in his throat.

"*You're* going to hang the chandelier?"

She crossed her arms and frowned up at him. "Yes, *I'm* going to hang the chandelier."

Quinn rubbed his hand over his jaw. "Is it electric?"

"Of course," she said stiffly.

He nodded slowly and shoved his hands into his pockets. His jacket had been tossed a while ago, and she had to admit the crisp white cotton emphasized his bronzed skin and dark hair. She read his expression and knew he doubted her abilities.

"You can watch and see how it's done, if you'd like," she said jauntily, opening the door and walking back into the house. She heard Quinn muttering something as he followed her inside.

She was careful not to trip on the protective blankets the painters had placed on the stairs as she made her way to the master bedroom. So much progress had already been made, and Holly loved the way the new banister gleamed and was smooth beneath her fingers. The wide-plank floors had been refinished and creaked in a homey way that her condo in the city didn't. At the top of the staircase was an arched stained-glass window that cast a soft glow as the sun beat through the pane.

"I meant to tell you, I think you did a great job with this room," Quinn said as he followed her into the bedroom.

"Thank you. I'm really happy with it," she said, her gaze going from his to the pale blue walls. It was one of her favorite colors—it was lighter than the ocean, but breezy enough to make her think of the beach. She had ordered a mahogany, four-poster bed that had simple, clean lines. And she'd found a pale blue duvet cover with white piping around the edges. It was elegant without being fussy. Once the house sold, she'd bring back the linens and make use of them in her condo. On either side of the king-sized bed were coordinating nightstands. Lamps with white silk shades that would complete the look were set to arrive in a few weeks. It was a style that she...or any prospective buyer would like. She had worked with this particular staging company countless times at Martin Laurence, and they'd been more than happy to help her out again.

The fireplace was original to the home, but after much deliberation she and Quinn had decided to turn this wood-burning fireplace to a gas one. She knew that homeowners would probably prefer the modern convenience in the bedroom, so a realistic gas insert was placed in the hearth, framed by the original antique mantel. She was pleased with the result.

"Though, I don't really agree with you having all these floors refinished so soon in the project," he said, stuffing his hands into his pockets.

Here we go. "Can you ever give a compliment without following it up with criticism?"

"Well, come on, you're a senior designer. You know this was a pretty risky thing to do with all the trades still working. What if the guys drop tools or fixtures all over your floors?"

"I had to make the call to pull this reno together as fast as possible. That meant doing some things ahead of schedule. Your guys assured me they'd be careful — or don't you think your people are capable of that?" she said with a smirk, as

his jaw tightened. She turned away from him to pick up the ladder that was leaning against the wall.

"You want me to install that chandelier for you, Holly?" Quinn asked with a sigh as she walked over and positioned the ladder under the ceiling medallion.

"No thanks," she said, looking up at the wires hanging out of the ceiling. "Wouldn't want you to get your pretty-boy clothes all dirty," she said with a wink. And then her stomach fluttered erratically as he laughed and approached her.

"I think I can manage," he said dryly.

Here we go. "Nope, I've got it. I can install a chandelier with my eyes closed, but thanks for the offer." She had done this many times, even though she was sure Quinn assumed she had no idea what she was doing. When she started out at Martin's firm, she had to do tons of grunt work, and on smaller projects with tight deadlines everyone had to pitch in to get the job done. She ignored Quinn's exaggerated sigh as she carefully climbed the ladder with the small crystal chandelier. She was dying to see how this would look in here. It would be the final touch to the room—the jewelry on the little black dress.

"Holly, I could probably do this twice as fast as you, and I'm a lot taller," said Quinn, trying to sound patient.

"I'm more than capable of standing on a ladder and hooking up a light, okay? Are you afraid that I'll lose my footing, being the female that I am, and then you'll have to catch me?" She laughed. There was way too much testosterone in the house with all these male workers. The whole mouse debacle had clearly given them a deluded sense of superiority. Well, mouse-fearing or not, she was more than capable of hanging this thing.

She found herself smiling at his deep chuckle as she reached an appropriate height and rested the chandelier on the top of the ladder.

"Yeah. That's exactly what I think. But go ahead. Being down here while you're up there definitely has its perks." She felt him brace one of his arms on the ladder. Quinn the flirt was very charming.

Holly reached for the wires that were dangling from the ceiling. Then she looked at the ones hanging out of the chandelier. She cursed herself for buying vintage this time. The wires weren't marked like the ones she usually dealt with. She peered down at Quinn. She might actually need his help. He raised his eyebrow, then smiled. He looked like a giant lion ready to pounce on his lunch. No way. Maybe she'd wait until Quinn went home and then ask one of the electricians later.

"Well, aren't you going to ask me why?" Quinn prodded.

"Why what?" She let out an exasperated sigh as she continued to study the wires. It was hopeless. But she had to pretend that she knew what she was doing while he was here.

"Why I like being down here while you're up there," Quinn said, smile still attached to his voice.

"Why, Quinn?" she asked absently, still tinkering at the top of the ladder. Seriously, she never knew the man talked this much.

"Because the view of your—"

"Mouse!" Holly screamed as a hideous black creature scurried across the room. Quinn turned to look where she was pointing, and Holly's foot slipped as she craned to follow the direction of the mouse. She crashed to the ground with a mortifying unladylike thud.

"Oh God, Holly, are you okay?" Quinn asked, kneeling beside her. Holly glared at him as she rubbed her ankle, trying to catch her breath. Her entire body throbbed from the impact of the fall. She looked over at the poor chandelier, which had crashed to the ground alongside her. Pieces of crystal sparkled as they littered the ground.

"I'm fine. But my gorgeous chandelier is toast," she managed to grumble. She had never in her life fallen off a ladder. And now, here, with Quinn, she had to embarrass herself like this?

"Yup, looks like it," he said, nodding as he looked at the mess.

Holly frowned, remembering the original cause of her current situation. "What about the mouse?"

"Oh, he's gone. In fact, you may have scared away the whole lot of them with that crash."

"Thanks."

"Let me look at your ankle," he said, laughter still in his voice. He shoved her hand away when she wouldn't budge. Holly smacked his hand and shot him another dirty look. And then she made the mistake of looking at his mouth, and then up into those blue eyes that weren't laughing anymore. They were filled with such concern that her voice, her argument, was stuck in her throat.

"Sweetheart, I'm so sorry," he said softly.

She refused to acknowledge the delicious thrill at the endearment that seemed to drip from his mouth like honey.

"Don't worry about it. I can take care of myself," she whispered as she touched her ankle.

He sighed roughly. "You're mad because I didn't catch you, aren't you?"

She shook her head. "*No*, of course not."

"For the record, I'm sorry," he said, his voice deep and husky. "Here, let me help you over to the window seat," he added, positioning his arms under her knees. She shooed him away.

"I am fully capable of standing on my own, Quinn. Besides, how do I know you won't drop me?" she asked. His jaw clenched. There was no way she was letting him pick her up…and be snuggled against that hard chest, his strong arms pressing her against him.

She slowly tried standing on the other ankle as Quinn cursed under his breath and stood beside her. "I'm sure I weigh considerably more than the lollipop women you're used to," she said under her breath. *That was the nickname she and Claire had come up with!* Why didn't her brain filter that out before her mouth ejected it?

She hobbled over to the window seat with Quinn's hand clamped around her upper arm. She knew there was no point in telling him that wasn't necessary.

"Lollipop women?" His eyebrows were bunched together.

Holly inhaled sharply. And then quickly tried to save face. "Hmm, what? I didn't say anything," Holly said, darting her eyes away from his.

"Yes, you did. You said 'lollipop women.'"

Holly pursed her lips.

"Quinn, obviously we have a situation with the mice that needs to be dealt—"

"Spill it, Holly."

How could she have actually let that slip? As if she hadn't felt humiliated enough today. "You know," she said, waving her hand around in the air and sitting down once they'd reached the seat. Quinn yanked off his tie while she fumbled with the right words to explain a silly old nickname.

"What are you doing?" Holly asked when he unbuttoned the top button of his shirt.

"Stripping," he said dryly as he placed his tie on the corner of the window seat. "I hate ties," he grumbled, rolling up his sleeves, baring strong, tanned forearms. How was it possible that he could look even better as the day went on? His crisp white shirt stretched across his broad chest as he rolled his shoulders.

"Well, so about this mouse—"

"Nice try. Back to the lollipop women. I didn't know there was…another species of woman."

Holly gave him a stern look. He was practically laughing already and she hadn't even started explaining yet. "It's really a stupid story. You won't be interested."

"No, no. I can bet ten bucks I'm really going to like this," he said, grinning and folding his arms in front of him.

"Fine, if you must know. Lollipop women was a nickname that Claire and I came up with one night, a long time ago, after way too many glasses of her father's hidden stash of brandy… It's silly really."

Quinn just smiled at her, his face almost boyish as he waited for further explanation. It was as though he knew how embarrassing this was going to be. "Spill it, Holly."

Holly rolled her eyes. "You're such a kid. Fine. The term 'lollipop women' refers to your many girlfriends. You see, we realized that all the women you dated had these giant heads." She raised her arms and made the shape of a circle around her head, while Quinn continued to stare at her, his eyes wide and his mouth twitching, trying to hold back his laughter.

Holly shook her head. "Anyway, these giant heads of theirs were partly due to their overinflated egos, and partly due to way too much hairspray and teasing…so…" she faltered and faked a cough before continuing, "so…these giant lollipop heads were placed on these long, skinny figures that looked just like a lollipop stick." She folded her hands in her lap and waited.

Quinn shot his head back and howled with pure, unadulterated hilarity. Holly stared at him. She had never heard him laugh so loud. After a few seconds she actually found herself smiling, despite her embarrassment. That is, until the laughter continued, and he was actually clutching his sides and gasping for air.

This was getting a little ridiculous. She crossed her arms and glared at him. His laughter slowed to a soft chuckle, tenderness flickering across his eyes. He sat beside her on the window seat, shaking his head.

"Holly, you kill me. I never know what is going to come out of that sexy mouth of yours." He held up his hand before she could interrupt. Her heart pounded with successively louder thuds as his eyes wandered over her in a very slow, very appreciative stare and the word *sexy* echoed in her mind. When his eyes lingered on her breasts and she felt herself immediately respond, she crossed her arms before her. The man was way too confident.

"I'm glad you find me intriguing," she began haughtily, but stopped speaking as he leaned across and cupped the back of her head.

"Holly," he began in a voice so throaty and seductive that all she could do was stare into his eyes, that had turned a darker, deeper shade of blue. She was in way over her head,

A RISK WORTH TAKING

feeling a little crazy as her mouth went dry and a decadent, dangerous heat swam through every inch of her body.

. . .

"Hey, Quinn!" Jake's loud, booming voice, followed by his approaching footsteps, jarred Quinn back into reality. His eyes dropped to Holly's mouth as he slowly eased his hand from her neck. He had never wanted to kiss another woman so badly in his life. She was this crazy mix of sarcasm and vulnerability and altogether sexiness. He couldn't get enough of her. Her lips were still parted, and he knew she was just as turned on as he was. And hell, he'd barely touched her.

"Quinn, where the hell are you?" Jake called again.

Quinn cursed under his breath and pushed himself up off the window seat. His brother had the worst timing. Just because Jake had been working here almost every day, he didn't have to act like he owned the damn place. And did he have to yell like a toddler searching for his mother?

Jake appeared in the doorway. "Oh, here you are."

"I thought you were having lunch? And you shouldn't be yelling, there's a baby in the house," Quinn said, trying to appear civil, when in reality he wanted to tell Jake to get lost.

"Finished. Ooh, right, the baby. Sorry, Holly," Jake said, wincing and turning to look at her.

"No problem, Jake," Holly said, standing up without looking at Quinn. "Well, I better get back to work," Holly said and limped across the room. Quinn cursed himself again for missing her when she fell. It was that crazy scream about the mouse that had him looking in the other direction. Quinn followed her into the closet. She began sorting through a pile of stacked boxes. Or pretending to, by the looks of things.

"Careful you don't fall in," he said when she practically shoved her head into the box to avoid him. "Holly?" She finally looked up at him, raising her eyebrows. "Are you sure your ankle is okay?"

She nodded, giving him a stiff smile.

"Okay, I'll see you tomorrow then," he said. He could feel Jake sniffing around, just waiting to catch a hint of something between him and Holly. He made a mental note to see if there was a project out of town he could send Jake to for the duration of Holly's stay.

"Oh, actually, I need to do some shopping for when I stage the house, so I won't be around tomorrow," she said, pulling out a bunch of bubble wrap from inside the box.

Quinn's eyes traveled over her, his gut clenching into a knot as her shirt tightened over her breasts. And then he pictured her in that shirt upstairs. Dammit. She definitely wasn't one of the "lollipop women."

"I'll probably be gone all day, but if something comes up just call me on my cell phone, okay?"

"Why don't I come with you?" *Whoa.* Did he really just offer to go shopping with Holly? Judging by the sound of Jake's loud scoff behind him, he did. Panic tore through him. He hated shopping. Abhorred it. The last woman he'd been shopping with was Christine, and he swore he'd never do it again. And yet here he was, asking Holly if he could go shopping with her. And Ella. The thought of Ella cheered him up a bit. He had missed her this week.

Jake slapped him on the back. "That sounds like a great day, buddy. Holly, Quinn just loves shopping. I have to practically haul him out of the mall."

Quinn knew his face was heating up. Right now he'd rather step on a rusty nail than have to endure Jake witnessing his humiliation. He turned to glare at his brother. His death stare must have had some effect, because Jake's stupid grin faltered a notch or two.

Holly pierced through the bubbles in the plastic wrap as he waited like a moron for her to answer. It was on the fifth pop that she nodded. "Are you sure you're up for a day of shopping with a baby in tow?"

Quinn quickly spoke before his brother had a chance to. "Nine?"

"Sure, see you at nine."

"So, looks like things with Holly are strictly professional," Jake said wryly as he merged onto the highway.

Quinn shot him a dirty look. "They are."

"Funny, when I walked in the room it looked like you were ready to inhale her face."

"We were having a conversation," Quinn bit back. He stared out the window pensively as his brother weaved in and out of traffic at Jake-speed.

"About what, lipstick?"

Quinn clenched the armrest. "Can you just drive and stop acting like a pansy?"

"I'm sure by *now* you've told her about Christine," Jake said, shooting him a look that showed no sign of even remotely processing what Quinn had just said.

"Jake, why don't you worry about yourself. Last time I got a glimpse of your love life, you were skulking out of the Stop and Drop at four a.m.," Quinn said, reminding his brother of his own dysfunctional relationships.

"That's a low blow, buddy."

"Well, then stop talking to me about Holly, and stop mentioning my damn ex-wife."

"I'm just seeing if you've gotten over blaming yourself for what happened."

Quinn didn't say anything and looked out the passenger window.

"Quinn?"

"It *was* my fault," Quinn spat out. He hated thinking about what happened with Christine. No matter what Jake said, no matter that they'd both moved on, he'd always feel responsible.

"It wasn't your fault. Christine only wanted your money."

"Leave her alone," Quinn said through clenched teeth.

"Christine married you for your money. The first moment that her faith in you was tested, she failed."

"Either drop the damn subject or pull over so I can walk," Quinn bit out.

"Fine. You should still tell Holly."

"Shut up, Jake."

"Sure. You have fun tomorrow. I know how much you *love* shopping."

Quinn grabbed the door handle. It took all of his self control not to pitch himself out of the car. "Pull over, I'm walking."

Jake stopped grinning. "Okay, okay. Relax," he said, turning up the volume on the stereo.

Chapter Six

"I cannot believe I'm at a flea market," Quinn grumbled as he pushed Ella's stroller around a pile of mud. Despite the morning rain that had left the grounds soppy and muddy, the market was filled with eager collectors and deal hunters.

"I didn't twist your arm, Quinn. *You* volunteered to come along," Holly answered as she stopped at a table of kitchen-ware and picked up an antique tin coffee pot. She examined it as Quinn sighed loudly beside her. To her surprise, shopping with Quinn was very entertaining. He loved to tease, and he had a sharp sense of humor. She'd been excited that he had offered to come along with them, and this morning she had actually spent an extra two minutes in the shower to shave her legs. And yes, she was wearing her favorite jeans. And yes, at the last minute, when she'd looked at her muddy running shoes, she had decided to wear her cute black boots instead. But no, she was not going to acknowledge what any of that meant.

"I thought you meant shopping at a mall. You know, like regular people do," Quinn said, looking around.

Holly swallowed a laugh. "Flea markets are great places to find unique things and get a deal. Besides, I want the house to have that family, country vibe going for it. A flea market is the perfect place to find that kind of stuff!" She lifted the rusty lid on the coffee pot and looked inside. It really was charming and would look great on the beadboard-backed open shelving in the kitchen. "Look at this. Doesn't it make you think of a lone cowboy out on the prairie making himself some coffee over an open fire?"

Quinn scowled, looking back and forth from the pot to her. "No. It makes me think it's a rusted piece of junk that some con man is trying to sell to make a quick buck off naive people."

"Oh, yeah. A real con man," Holly said, bopping her head in the direction of the frail, elderly man sitting in a lawn chair beside his merchandise. "Hold on to your wallet, Quinn, he might tackle you," she added dryly as she approached the man with a compassionate smile.

"Hello there, sir," Holly said with a bright smile.

The man sat forward in his lawn chair, his eyes squinting as he took her in. "Hello, Missy, see something you like?"

"Well, I do like this coffee pot, but I couldn't find a price," Holly said, reaching across the table. She gave Quinn a see-isn't-he-sweet look as he stood beside her with the stroller. Quinn rolled his eyes.

Holly stiffened slightly as the man gave her a thorough once-over. "Seventy-five dollars," he said, slapping his leg.

Holly gasped and ignored Quinn's snort and Ella's cackle. Ella seemed to have taken on the role of Quinn's sidekick.

"*Seventy-five dollars?* That seems a little steep." Holly knew that other vendors had identical ones going for around twenty-five dollars.

The man shook his bald head, leaning back in his chair. "This is a real antique, sugar, if you knew something about antiques."

"Well, I do know a lot, actually." Holly refused to look in Quinn's direction, but she could practically feel the jubilation radiating from his body.

"Now, sweetie, maybe if you ask your husband real nice, he can buy it for you," the man said.

Holly glared at the old man, who suddenly looked as greedy as an old dog stealing a steak. She squared her shoulders and lifted her chin. "Look. I don't have to ask anyone."

"Oh, now, sugar, I'll buy it for you," Quinn said with an exaggerated drawl, putting his arm around her.

Holly turned to glare at Quinn, but the laughter in his eyes and the mischievous grin that transformed his masculine features made her forget the man's patronizing assumptions. Quinn's hard body locked beside hers, and she forced herself not to think about how good he felt. She was pressed up against his side and could smell his fresh cologne. Quinn gave her shoulder a squeeze, and she shot him an aggravated look. She was never going to hear the end of this.

"Thank you, *sweetie,* but I know when I'm being ripped off." The old man shrugged and put it back on the table.

"Nope. I wanna buy it," Quinn said, moving away from her and picking up the coffee pot. The old man rose with the energy of a child and scurried over to the table.

"No, you are not buying it," Holly said, firmly taking the coffee pot from him and setting it back down on the table.

"Yes, I *am*," Quinn said, his jaw tightening as he reached for his wallet and pulled out a few bills. The man smiled.

Holly glared at both of them. "You are not buying that for me, Quinn."

"Aw now, don't be so difficult," the man chortled.

Holly stared in disbelief as Quinn handed the man seventy-five dollars.

"Yeah, sweetie, stop being so difficult," Quinn said, with an edge to his smile.

Holly mouthed the word *bastard* to Quinn.

He burst out laughing, then picked up the coffee pot again.

"Here. It's a gift," Quinn said sharply, shoving the coffee pot in her direction.

"I don't need you to buy—"

"It's a piece of tin, not a diamond."

"Oh, well, when you put it so nicely—"

"Take the damn pot, Holly. Seeing as I'm so old anyway, it may be my last gift to you." Quinn's eyes locked onto hers as he shoved the coffee pot into her hands.

"Thank you," she said stiffly.

"You're welcome," he replied, and she saw the corner of his mouth twitch.

"I never knew you were such a romantic," she said, placing the pot in the compartment under the stroller.

"Well, maybe if you'd stop being so difficult, you could see that I really am a romantic at heart," he said, his voice thick with laughter. Holly paused. What was that supposed to mean? She rose to meet his gaze, but thankfully he wasn't even looking at her.

He was busy playing peek-a-boo with Ella.

• • •

"I'm starved. Is there anywhere to eat at this junk festival?" Quinn asked two hours later. He was watching as Holly tried to cram a bag containing an antique quilt with farm animals and flowers into the packed storage compartment under the stroller. She said she was going to hang it in Ella's bedroom when they got back home. By "home," she meant Toronto, and that put him in a foul mood. He tried to shake it off. She was infuriating and intoxicating.

He was surprised to find that Holly was such a romantic. After walking around with her and having her explain the relevance of items he would have normally overlooked, he could see why they appealed to her. She was a dreamer and liked imagining the stories behind the pieces she found. She had spent a good ten minutes *ooh*ing and *ahh*ing over a vintage drafting table, and when he'd offered to buy it for her, she'd vehemently refused. He knew there was no way she'd accept his offer, so he didn't bother asking again.

As much as her independence irritated him, he understood it—and admired her for it. It also made him think of his ex, who had always relied on him for everything. Hell, everyone relied on him. Except, Ella and Holly made all of it seem so easy. Ella made him forget everything he'd done wrong—she made him think that she could be his second chance. And Holly, well…Holly was becoming difficult to ignore on every single level.

"Me, too. They're serving food over there," Holly said and pointed to the large white tent with flags that read FOOD, DRINK, DESSERT in bold red print. People were walking in and out with trays of food.

"*You're* going to eat in a tent?" He glanced at the plastic chairs and tables and then back at Holly.

Holly turned and put her hands on her hips, frowning up at him. Quinn let his eyes flicker over her body. Very, very nice. Being around her was torture—sweet torture. All he wanted to do was kiss her. But the thought of kissing her led to thoughts of making love to·her, which made it impossible to concentrate.

"You're very funny," she muttered as she pushed the stroller toward the tent. He gave her cute backside one last look before catching up to her.

"This smells good," he said, standing beside her in line. The sweet aroma of smoky barbecue greeted them and his stomach growled. They read the menu on a large white board above the cashier station.

"What do you feel like?" he asked, bending down to speak close to her ear. God, she smelled good, like spring-time mixed with pure woman. He straightened up before he was tempted to kiss the fragrant skin he'd been so close to. The crowd was loud and boisterous. Ella joined in the noise, squealing and pointing to baked goods that were on display, her stroller jostling with the movement.

"I don't know. Coffee and a barbecue chicken sandwich?"

"Sounds good to me. Why don't you and Ella go find a table and I'll bring the food over." The look in her eyes said she was about to argue with him. He didn't even have a remote idea of what he'd just said that could cause her to object.

"Well—"

"Does everything have to be a debate with you?"

She raised her eyebrows, her hand flying to her chest. *"Me?"*

He nodded. "Yes. You."

"Of course not. Fine. We'll go sit. Let me give you some money—"

So that was it. "You are not going to give me five dollars for a sandwich and a coffee, okay? Tomorrow, you can buy me something that's worth five dollars, and then the world will be right again, and you'll be able to sleep at night, okay?"

She shook her head. "That's not it at all—you already overpaid for that coffee pot, I thought—"

"Can you just let me get lunch?" She stared at him for a long moment, and he realized this was the first woman he'd ever met who actually didn't expect him to pay for something.

"Fine, thank you. I brought some food for Ella, but maybe she'd like a muffin," she said, peering at the display of baked goods stacked in a wire basket.

Quinn nodded, relieved that this wasn't going to become a long, drawn-out argument.

Holly turned the stroller and then stopped. "Oh, and ask if it's all-natural—"

"Go," Quinn groaned.

She nodded, and he actually thought she was going to leave. "Just make sure there's no hydrogenated—"

"Seriously? Can you just get a table?"

She frowned and then pushed the stroller away in search of a table. Quinn made a mental note to ask the cashier whether or not the muffins had hydrogenated oil and if they were all-natural.

. . .

"What is with the weather this fall?" Holly asked, looking out the window of her SUV. They were on their way back to Red River after what had to be the best day she'd had in a long, long time. Just as they were packing up the car, a downpour hit. The rainstorm was so violent that they could barely see the pavement in front of them. Luckily the country roads weren't heavily trafficked.

"I know. I heard we've broken records." Quinn was driving in case she needed to take care of Ella on the hour-long drive home. "I like your car," he said as he toyed with the radio before shutting it off.

"Thanks—it's for show, really," she said with a slight smile. Right now, work and Toronto felt so far away. For a second—and not for the first time today—she imagined that this was what her life could be like. That Quinn could be the man in her and Ella's life, that they could be their own family. It felt good to have Quinn here, to be bundled in the car with him beside her, making her feel warm and safe. She blinked away the emotion in her eyes. Thoughts like that were dangerous. Dreams that relied on other people had never panned out for her, and she wasn't strong enough to lose again.

Holly stared straight ahead as the windshield wipers frantically swished across the window. The rain was coming down so hard that even at the fastest setting, the windshield filled with rain faster than the wipers could clear it. Yet there wasn't even the smallest doubt in her mind that Quinn would get them home safely.

"Thank you for coming with us," Holly whispered, shooting him a sideward glance. She felt a jolt of excitement as he broke into a wide smile.

"I had a nice time, too. It felt good to get away from work for a day," he said as he merged the SUV onto the old country highway.

"Is this a busy time of year for your company?" Holly asked, wanting to know more about how he'd grown the business.

He nodded. "It's just a lot of timing issues right now. We're sort of in a race against the clock. We have a condo project going up, and that foundation needs to be poured before winter hits, but the crazy rain this fall has slowed everything down. If the weather eases up a bit, we'll have to push ahead. I'm just waiting for that break."

"Well, at least when my place is done you'll have some free time," Holly said with a forced laugh. She knew he'd been going above and beyond for her. Really, dealing with mouse issues in her house was the last thing he needed to be wasting time on.

"There's something I've wanted to tell you," he said with a rough sigh. Her mouth went dry at his tone and the sudden tension that infused his body. "What happened that first morning—you're wrong, Holly," he said in a low voice, quickly turning to look into her eyes. She didn't expect him to explain anything to her. It had hung between them, but Holly had never brought it up again, because she knew that would be like opening a can of worms. "You couldn't be further from the truth in thinking I'm still in love with Christine. I'm not. I never was. We got married because I felt we had to, not because I wanted to," he said, his expression grim.

Holly's heart constricted. *He wasn't in love with Christine? He never was?* She didn't say anything as she clenched her hands in her lap. This shouldn't matter. Those words shouldn't matter. When he turned to look at her, his blue eyes had darkened—and just as they had ten years earlier, they reminded her of the pure, indigo night sky of the open country.

Holly swallowed past the cowardice constricting her throat. "What exactly do you mean by that?"

His jaw tightened. "I was never in love with her," he said, his voice barely above a low whisper, his eyes focused on the road ahead. Every second that ticked by kept her immobilized in the realization that he'd never loved Christine.

She licked her lips, feeling her mouth go dry. "Oh."

"And I want to make you understand, but I don't know if I can." His voice was a delicious, deep whisper.

"Okay," she said finally, not sure if he was going to continue.

"Okay, then," he repeated, jaw tight.

Holly cleared her throat. "So, you're not in love with Christine."

He shook his head and turned quickly, his eyes falling to her lips before they focused on the road again.

Holly swallowed hard. "And you never were."

He shook his head again.

Holly took a deep breath, unable to stop herself from repeating the facts, reminding herself of why she could not let this go. "But you did sleep with her. Right after I left. Right after we kissed. After you told me you had feelings for me, too."

His jaw clenched, and for a second Holly thought he was

A Risk Worth Taking

going to justify or deny. But Quinn wasn't the type of guy who lied and made excuses. "Yup, I did. But I also told you that you were too young. You were eighteen and you left. I never believed that you would really come back."

The admission hung between them, and Holly felt the sting of it in her heart. She tried to look braver and stronger than she felt. A part of her wanted to remind him, and herself, that none of this should matter. Who Quinn had been with, who he was with now, was completely irrelevant. She blinked a few times and finally got the words out. "I would have," she whispered, tears clogging her throat. "I guess this is all irrelevant now, since I'm leaving in five weeks, anyway. But I guess I still don't get why you married someone you didn't love?"

The silence stretched for several minutes. Holly was torn between staring at his stony profile and watching the road ahead.

"We got married because she was pregnant."

• • •

Quinn stared ahead intently as the yellow divider lines on the road disappeared beneath the onslaught of rain. He never should have taken Holly's advice on taking the scenic mountainside route. On the best days, it was a drive that required lots of concentration. On nights like this one, even concentration could not guarantee a safe arrival home. He gripped the steering wheel tighter as he felt the car shifting with the strong winds. He glanced in the rearview, amazed that Ella could sleep through the noise.

Holly always could rattle him. Somewhere inside he

knew that he wanted to confide in her, but he wasn't exactly sure why. He hated talking about this. But he owed her an explanation. And he needed her to believe him when he said he never loved Christine. If he were completely honest with himself, he'd admit the real reason he didn't want to tell her was fear that she'd look at him differently. She'd know he'd screwed up. Badly.

"It was a painful time and I made a lot of mistakes," he admitted after a few minutes, cringing at how loud he sounded in the silence of the car.

"Sometimes the line between right and wrong isn't so easy to see," said Holly. "We all make the best choices we can at the time."

Something clenched inside him. He didn't know if it was because what she said hit home or because he detected that she wasn't judging him.

"I don't want to make excuses for myself, Holly. I let Christine down." He stared ahead, concentrating on the road and swallowing his feelings. But he had to tell her.

"So you got married because of the baby?" Holly asked when he didn't speak.

He nodded. "But I didn't love her, and she didn't love me. She thought she did. And she was so damn happy about the baby," he said roughly. "I didn't want the baby, Holly. I resented Christine. I was angry that I was put in that position. It was just a casual relationship. We were both young—there weren't supposed to be strings. And then everything happened at the same time. It felt like my world was crumbling around me. My parents died, and I was left with a business on the edge of bankruptcy. Jake took off, Evan was in med school, and I was left here, trying to keep everything afloat.

I caved. I sold the family house to pay for Evan's school—I never told him about the debt in the business until much later. I basically sold everything I had, and Christine and I rented a crappy little place downtown. I worked my ass off and was never around for her. But I think the worst thing was that I was angry—I didn't want a baby. I was too young, too in debt, and I didn't love my child's mother. What kind of man doesn't want their own child? She had called me for help the morning she miscarried. But I was so self-centered, I didn't answer the phone. I thought she was just calling to rail into me for something. Who doesn't answer a call from their pregnant wife? I found out after it was all over. She miscarried in the hospital, all alone. I wasn't there. If I had answered my phone, I could have gotten her to the hospital in time. She may not have lost the baby. I felt like a monster. I failed Christine. I was selfish and stupid, and the thought that our baby died without ever knowing that I loved him—"

"You don't know that you could have saved the baby. You can't take that kind of blame," she said, interrupting him. "I know you, better than you think. And I know, without a doubt, that had your baby been born, you would have loved him more than yourself. I know what kind of man you are, and not for one second do I think there'd be a better father out there. You are the man that wants to take care of everything. You want to fix things for everyone. And for once in your life, you couldn't. You couldn't make everything right, and you're blaming yourself." She reached out and put her hand on his thigh, her voice trailing off.

Her hand on his leg was gentle, reassuring, and it was like she reached inside of him and tugged on that piece of his heart he'd been hiding. He didn't know how she was able to do this. To see through him, to figure him out, to forgive him and absolve him of mistakes he'd made. He blinked past the wetness that stung the back of his eyes. He glanced over at her and was shaken. Because as the three of them sat in the car, lost in the pain of his memories, he wondered how things would have turned out if that had been Holly.

Quinn cleared his throat. There was no point in looking back and wishing for things that couldn't happen. Ella's cry broke the sudden silence, and it was a poignant reminder of what he'd said no to. Quinn squared his shoulders, reining in the unusual emotions that were encompassing his thoughts.

"What are you doing?" he gasped.

Holly had unbuckled her seat belt and was leaning into the back of the SUV.

"Grabbing a pacifier. She'll terrorize us if I don't find it," she mumbled, nowhere near her seat anymore.

"You can't take off your seat belt while I'm driving on a cliff in a raging storm!"

She ignored him and continued rummaging around the backseat.

"Holly, hurry up." He rounded a turn and started on a downward descent from the mountain.

"Stop being such an old grouch," she called out over her shoulder.

"I'm not old."

"There! All done," she said with a smile as she sat back down and re-buckled her seat belt. Ella stopped crying. "That should buy us twenty minutes."

"No pressure," he said dryly.

He took the turnoff to her street a few minutes later,

then pulled into the dark driveway. He wanted to ask her so many things. And he didn't want this day to be over—another day closer to when she'd leave forever.

Holly was fishing in her purse for her keys. *Dammit.* Why did it always feel like he never had enough time with her? The porch lights filtered through the car window, illuminating the car enough that he could see her clearly.

"Thanks again, Quinn," she said, shooting him a sidelong smile as she gathered her purse and belongings. They were back to pretending nothing had happened.

"I'll carry Ella in for you," he said, glancing back at the sleeping baby.

"No, that's—"

"Please, I don't mind," he said hoarsely as he unbuckled his seat belt.

"Okay. Thanks," she said, shocking him with her easy acquiescence. They were being much too polite.

"Considering how hard the rain is coming down, I think I'll leave all my purchases in the car tonight," Holly said. "I hope they'll be safe."

He couldn't resist. "I really think that if a thief broke into a Lexus, he wouldn't be doing it for that junk in the back."

"It's not junk," she grumbled.

Quinn opened his door and cursed as he stepped in a giant pothole of muddy water, the rain soaking him instantly. He made a mental note to mention to Holly that the driveway needed paving. Maybe he'd hire someone to pave the driveway at his own expense. He'd deal with Holly's wrath over that later.

He came around to the passenger side just as Holly was

emerging. She handed him a blanket for Ella.

"You go inside. I'll get her. No point in both of us getting soaked," he said, opening the back door. He unbuckled Ella and gently pulled her into his arms, wrapping the blanket around her. She murmured softly, then settled against him with the complete trust only a baby could have.

Quinn made his way down the uneven path and joined Holly on the porch. Holly jiggled the lock and jerked the door open, stepping inside silently as he followed. She flicked on a light and turned to look at him.

"Do you want me to hold her?" she whispered, looking at Ella, who seemed to be perfectly content snoozing on his shoulder.

Quinn shook his head. Then he looked up at Holly and lost all sense of self-preservation. His mind emptied of the reasons they couldn't be together, and refilled with all the reasons they should be. Holly and Ella were bringing out feelings…powerful, protective feelings he couldn't ignore. Holly's large eyes were on him, and he could swear he read the same longing in her eyes. He knew she felt it. His eyes wandered over her face as she watched him. He looked at her hair falling in soft waves around her shoulders. The stubborn chin. The full lips. He took it all in, memorized it, cherished it. He wanted her. He wanted to be the man in Holly and Ella's life.

"I'd invite you in, but—"

He shook his head. He was going to say the words that he'd wanted to since she told him she was selling the house. "Have you thought about staying here?" He held his breath as she placed her coat on the chair in the entry.

She didn't look at him when she answered, "What would

we do here? I have an amazing career, stable income—"

"Work for me," he blurted out, carefully shifting Ella in his arms so she was snuggled warmly against his other shoulder. Holly working as an interior designer at his company had been an idea he'd been toying with for a few weeks. Was it selfishly motivated? Sure it was.

"We could use an interior designer on staff. Especially one with your credentials. We're going to be doing some more condo projects and corporate work. I think it would be a great fit."

She crossed her arms. "I can't. Moving back here is not an option for me."

"But you'd have a job. You'll have a flexible schedule, work from home, we have an excellent benefits package. You'd be back in the town you grew up in, the same house—"

Holly's eyes locked onto his, her expression silencing him "You don't understand. I *can't* move back here. It's not an option." There was something in her eyes that bothered him.

He frowned. "Why not?"

"I have a life in Toronto," she whispered. Her face had turned pale, and he could tell there was more than she was letting on.

"Yeah, but I bet you hardly get to see Ella. What if I told you I could offer you a position that would allow you to work from home most of the time? I mean, it's not Martin Laurence, but it's still—"

"Thank you. But I can't move back here, I can't live in this house." Her voice cracked, and he felt like a jerk. A few weeks ago, he'd called her cold for selling the house. Now, he knew. The vulnerability that she tried so desperately to hide was staring him in the face. Holly was afraid. This place was her old house, but everyone she loved was gone. The memories were haunting her. He felt powerless at seeing her pain. He hated thinking of Holly as alone, of having no one left to rely on. Yet she stood there proudly. Stoically. Her eyes held a pain he knew he'd never fully comprehend. Her chin trembled, and he knew she was blinking back tears, desperate to hold on to them. Because Holly hated showing weakness. He understood that. He could even admire it. Except when the pain was so strong that it threatened to destroy her. He wanted to shake her. He wanted to yell at her until she let it all out. He wanted her to trust him with her heartache.

"Did you ever think that maybe your grandparents would have wanted you to live here with Ella? That maybe Jennifer and Rick would have wanted—"

"Jennifer and Rick were going to live here. I was supposed to do this renovation for them. They should be here now, with Ella. I don't belong in this house anymore. I know you can't understand. You have family, you have Jake and Evan. I have no one."

"Don't say that," he bit out harshly. He wanted to add that she had him, but how could he, when their relationship was barely definable. "You have Ella."

"Now I have Ella. But I have no idea if she's going to grow up and hate me—"

"What the hell are you talking about?"

"I don't want to talk about this anymore. I'm tired. I have to get Ella to bed. Thanks for coming with us today," she said. Her eyes filled with tears as she reached out for Ella.

He shook his head. "The Holly I knew never would have

been afraid," he said gruffly, trying to illicit a reaction, trying to keep her talking any way he could. Her green eyes glittered and she tilted her chin up. "The girl that stood out on that porch ten years ago—"

"Was naive and trusting, and—"

"Was so goddamn sweet you took my breath away," he said, his voice coming out harsh and raspy. She backed up a step and her lower lip quivered. "Holly," he groaned, wanting to reach out and kiss her, hold her.

"Don't do this to me," she said, pointing a finger at him. "Not now. How do you think you'd feel if your only sibling died suddenly and left you with a baby? I had no one. No one," she gasped, tears filling her eyes, and it took all of Quinn's self control not to gather her in his arms. "Everyone I've ever loved is gone, and now I've got to figure out how the hell I'm going to keep my life and raise this little girl. And you think I'm going to move back here because you're offering me a job? Maybe a date? We've never been more than friends. You never even had the nerve to kiss me properly—"

"What?" Anger engulfed him at her accusation. *Didn't have the nerve to kiss her properly?*

"That's right," she said, nodding frantically.

"You were eighteen years old, for crying out loud. Forgive me if I had a policy against kissing teenagers."

"You were chicken."

Quinn's eyes were burning as he stared at her. "Chicken?"

She nodded vigorously. And then had the utter nerve to flap her arms. "As in *Bok, Bok.*"

"First you make me feel bad for everything you went through. And you know what? I do. And you know what else? I think you're the bravest damn woman I've ever met. You're the sexiest, hottest woman I've ever known and, hell, if you want me to kiss you, Holly, just ask."

He did get a bit of satisfaction when her mouth dropped open. But Ella stirred in his arms and Holly reached to get her. Conversation over.

"I think it's time I get her to bed," Holly whispered, looking flushed.

Quinn turned, ready to leave, but then paused. "I never kissed you the way I wanted to because I knew that if I did I wouldn't be able to stop. I wouldn't be able to get enough of you. And if I had thought for one second that you meant what you said that night, I would have come after you," he said. He turned, opened the door, and stepped out onto the porch, the damp night air cooling his hot skin. He took a deep breath and made a decision.

He wasn't going to lose Holly a second time.

Chapter Seven

"Holly?" Quinn's voice boomed over the hammering and drilling outside the kitchen. Holly frantically wiped at the splattering of pureed blueberries that Ella had just chucked all over her.

"In the kitchen," Holly answered, hating how her heart kicked into high gear just knowing Quinn was approaching. It had been well over a week since that night after the flea market, and she was still upset by the way they'd left things. When he'd said—in that deep, delicious voice—that the reason he'd never kissed her the way he wanted to was because he didn't think he'd be able to stop, she knew that if she hadn't been holding Ella, she would have walked straight into his arms and spent the rest of the night with him. And who knows what the repercussions of sleeping with him would have been. So she'd said good-bye and watched him leave. And then avoided him for over a week. It had been easy to do, since it seemed like he'd been avoiding her as well.

Alone in bed that night, she had entertained the idea of working as an interior designer for him. In a perfect world, it was the ideal solution. She would be able to keep her career, spend more time with Ella, live in this beautiful house in Red River surrounded by people she cared about…and Quinn. But the idea of that was terrifying. Because when it vanished…or when someone disappeared from her life, she'd have to deal with loss again. And she was done with that. Colleagues at work all had their own lives. She passed people on the street every day on her way to work, she sat beside strangers on the subway, rode the elevator with familiar faces, and, through it all, she was able to guard herself. That was the way she wanted it. Here…everyone knew everyone. And people cared about each other. The longer she stayed in Red River, the more time she spent with Quinn, the harder it became to think about leaving.

"What happened to you?"

Holly jerked her head up and a rush of heat infused her body as Quinn stood there, looking about as perfect as could be, grinning down at her obviously undignified state.

Ella squealed and banged her hands on the dirty tray in front of her. Quinn laughed and walked over. "How's my girl?" he asked, leaning down to give Ella a kiss on the top of her head. Holly stared at the exchange for a moment, frozen by the emotion that caught her by surprise, and then busied herself with cleaning Ella's mess.

"She's a bit grumpy. Barely slept last night," Holly said, trying to sound natural. Being so close to Quinn made her realize how much she hated being away from him.

"Yeah, you don't look so good. Can I take her out of

this thing?" Quinn asked as Ella extended her arms. Holly quickly smoothed her hair back from her face at his remark and then cursed herself for caring.

"Of course," Holly nodded, glancing down at her shirt. The blueberries were everywhere. Even if she crossed her arms, she would still look disgusting.

"Is she okay?" Quinn asked, smoothing Ella's fluffy hair off her forehead.

"I think so. I'm pretty sure she's getting a tooth," Holly said, softening her tone a bit as Ella smiled at Quinn.

"Oh, well, if you need anything during the night, you can call me," he said, his voice low and husky. Holly opened her mouth to answer, but then shut it again. "Did the window guys finish yet?" he asked.

"Window guys? I didn't know the window company was here," Holly said, trying to focus on their *professional* relationship.

"Remember, I told you I booked them for those basement windows? I saw their truck outside. Jake said he let them in a while ago," he added, glancing down at his phone. *Right.* Holly nodded slowly. He had mentioned that. But ugly little windows in the unfinished basement hadn't made her list of must-do renovation items. There was also the matter of the countertop company due to arrive at any moment to take measurements for the counter she had just changed her mind about. Both items would certainly spark an argument with Quinn.

Holly concentrated on the blueberry stains on the highchair and tried to ignore how adorable Ella looked nestled in Quinn's big arms. And how capable Quinn was with her, and how his face had lit up when he spoke to Ella. Holly sighed. "Yeah, I do remember seeing Jake walking toward the basement an hour or so ago. I was so busy with Ella that I didn't really pay any attention. I have the counter company due any minute," Holly said, clearing the remains of Ella's snack and tossing them into the garbage.

"They here to do the template?" Quinn asked as he tossed Ella into the air and caught her.

Holly gasped as Quinn threw Ella into the air again. Ella squealed with delight as he effortlessly caught her again. "I don't think that's very safe," Holly said, crossing her arms.

"I got her Holly. Trust me," he said, his voice softening as he looked into her eyes. Holly looked from him to Ella. Ella was poking him on the shoulder with a slobbery grin on her face. Holly forced herself to nod. She had seen people do this before and never witnessed a parent drop their child. *Trust me,* he said. Ella certainly did.

"Hi there," a voice called from the kitchen doorway. It was the men from the stone company.

"Hey, Brad," Quinn said, extending his hand.

"Good to see you, Quinn," the man said. "You, too, Holly."

"Hi, Brad," Holly said, spotting the rectangular sample of quartzite in his hand. She needed to get Quinn out of the room before he noticed it wasn't granite.

"So, you guys still on track to install this thing for next week?" Quinn asked, settling Ella on his hip. Holly wrung her hands together. Quinn needed to stop asking so many questions. Ella stared up at Quinn, listening intently as he spoke.

"Yes. John is just getting the equipment out of the car," he said, setting the stone sample on the table. Holly quickly walked over to it, hoping to hide it under the other samples and swatches of fabric and paint. She stifled a squeal of delight as she looked at the sample. It was gorgeous. She quickly buried it under a swatch of silk.

Quinn walked up and Holly pretended to organize the items on the table. She stood completely still as his large hand plucked the white silk away and tossed it aside. A waft of his aftershave floated toward her with the fabric and Holly's toes curled. How was it possible that even though he'd been working and sweating, he could smell so good?

"That's not the granite we chose last week," he said in a low voice, giving her a long look, inadvertently reminding her that she shouldn't be focusing on how delicious the man smelled. He was trying to control her renovation.

Holly straightened. "That's true. After we left the supplier's, I questioned whether or not granite was the way I wanted to go," she said, tapping her chin, trying to look casual as Quinn's frown deepened. "I'm not a fan of granite. Never have been. In fact, I never source granite for any of my clients—it's always marble or quartzite."

"That's great for your clients, but this isn't a project for Martin Laurence. This is a renovation in a rural area. Quartzite is way more expensive, Holly. A prospective buyer around here isn't going to pay more for the house because of quartz."

"I know that," Holly snapped.

"Then why would you put it in a house that you're flipping?"

Holly swallowed hard as she stared into his blue eyes. She glanced over at Brad, who was now setting up the digital template equipment with his partner. What was she going to say? How did she justify blowing several extra thousand dollars when she had spent every day insisting they stay on budget? She loved the look of this stone, but there was more to it than that. She didn't want to tell him that this slab of quartzite was almost identical to the marble countertop her grandmother had loved and circled from one of their magazine clippings.

"I think it's a signature design statement," she said stiffly.

"More like a signature bad decision, if you ask me," he said, shifting Ella to his other arm. "Stupid move," he said with a shake of his head. "Exactly what I'd expect from a designer," he muttered under his breath.

"That's so rude," she said, reaching out for Ella. Ella shook her head and buried it into Quinn's neck. Holly resisted the urge to stamp her foot. Was no one on her side? "Why do you care so much, anyway? This is my renovation."

"Well, I am the one running this operation, and the one who has to listen to your daily budget reminders."

"I happen to know you contractors—"

"Not a contractor, Holly," Quinn said, his perfect jaw tightening.

"Details, details," Holly said with a wave of her arm.

"Quinn, you in here?" Quinn muttered something under his breath, then turned in the direction of the voice. Two men filled the doorway.

"Hey, Rich, Peter, come on in," Quinn said, introducing Holly. Holly's stomach tightened. Why were all these people here, now, with Quinn around?

"So what do you think of those basement windows I mentioned?" Quinn asked, looking a little too confident. He knew exactly what they were going to say.

"Yeah, they gotta come out for sure," Peter said, nodding his head.

"Those windows have been here for years. Do they have to come out now?" Holly asked, ignoring Quinn's I-told-you-so stare.

"You're kind of playing with fire if they don't. All it takes is one big storm, and you could end up with a hell of a lot of flooding," he said, pulling out a paper with a written estimate.

Quinn sang a little *mmm hmm* under his breath and Holly's muscles tensed at the smug sound. "How much are we talking?" Quinn asked.

Peter handed him the quote. Holly quickly glanced at the bottom of the sheet for the final number. Her mouth went dry. It was almost the exact same number as the cost of the counters.

"How fast can you get this done?" Quinn asked, looking up from the quote to Peter.

"*If* I decide to get this done," Holly interjected, plucking the paper from his hand.

Richard and Peter looked at Quinn. "We can put a rush on it and have them installed before next weekend."

"Great. Well, once I decide, I can give you a call," Holly said, ushering them toward the door.

"We'll be calling you later today," Quinn said, completely contradicting her.

Holly turned to glare at him once the men had left. "I'm *not* deciding this right now," she said.

"You have to fix those windows," he said, frowning at her.

"We'll see," she said. He shook his head, his blue eyes glittering. Even angry, Quinn looked good. She needed to get him to leave.

"You must be busy. I appreciate you coming by, but no need to stay on my account," Holly said, reaching for Ella. This time, her niece finally decided to come to her. Holly hugged her tightly.

"I thought we could talk," he said, his tone softening slightly. Dangerously. It made her remember their chicken conversation. She was not going there.

"I don't think there's anything to talk about. I've got what? A few weeks left here?"

His jaw twitched and he didn't break her stare. She had hoped he'd stalk off, but instead he took a step closer.

"And Mrs. Jacobs is on her way over," Holly blurted out. She breathed an inward sigh of relief as panic shot across Quinn's face. She knew Quinn was not the type to appreciate the elderly woman's intrusion.

"Seriously?" he asked, backing up a step.

Holly nodded frantically. "Yup. Staying the whole afternoon. We're going to have a nice visit."

Quinn gave her a long look. One that started at the top of her head and then traveled her body at a rather leisurely pace until his eyes met hers again. "I think we both know you're the chicken, Holly," he said, before turning and walking out of the room. Holly held her breath until she heard the front door swing shut.

Holly paced back and forth between her flooded basement and the front door. She clutched her phone while she waited for Quinn to arrive. Less than half an hour ago, when she was heading into the basement to store some boxes, she'd been greeted by at least a foot of water flooding the basement floor.

It was the last thing she needed right now. Just last week, she'd proudly told Quinn that basement windows weren't a priority. What were the odds that the basement would flood? She had no idea how extensive the damage was going to be. There was still the remote chance that the windows weren't the reason there was a swimming pool in the basement. Maybe the water was leaking from the foundation… Of course, by texting Quinn and telling him there was an emergency at the house, she was playing into the whole damsel in distress image—and it drove her nuts. But she knew if she even attempted to deal with this mystery flooding without contacting him, he'd be livid. They were already on shaky ground. She felt guilty for even asking him to come over so late, especially since she'd heard Jake say earlier that Quinn was busy doing damage control on one of their condominium projects that had been flooded as well. But Quinn replied to her text less than two minutes later, saying he'd be right over.

The house had been buzzing with trades all day, even though it was a Saturday. There wasn't a room in the whole house that hadn't had someone working in it. The renovation was ahead of schedule, which was an absolute miracle. The kitchen had been installed, and even her prize quartzite counters had come in today. All that was needed was the backsplash and finishing touches, and the kitchen would be done. So far, she and Ella only had to stay at Claire's house a few nights, mostly during the sanding and floor refinishing. But since Holly had used only environmentally friendly

paints and products, it had been safe to live in the house during most of the renovation. The master bedroom was completely finished. She'd hung the white silk curtains today, and
was dreaming of relaxing in freshly washed cotton sheets on
the four-poster bed tonight. *After* taking a long, hot bath in
the new deep-soaker, stand-alone tub.

Claire and her parents had been looking after Ella for
the day. Claire had just called to say that she'd keep Ella
overnight because of the storm, which was good considering
Holly would be dealing with the basement flooding. It would
be their first night apart, but Holly trusted Claire completely. She couldn't think of any one of her friends back in Toronto that she'd feel comfortable leaving Ella with—not that
any of them would even offer. She had to admit that having
the entire day without having to care for Ella had helped
her get through a mountain of work. But it also made her
aware of how much she missed Ella, and that terrified her.
Since returning to Red River, she had spent every waking
moment with her niece. She loved the way Ella cuddled up
against her, the smile that she gave Holly every single morning when she went into her room. Of course she had loved
Ella as soon as she'd been born, but things were changing.
Emotions were stronger, harder to ignore. Everything was
changing now that they were back here, and it was Holly—
and not the nanny—who was Ella's constant companion.

The fall storm was pounding the house with rain and
hail. The wind was howling, and dusk was setting in with a
sense of foreboding. Holly sat on the basement stairs and
stared at the water again. She jumped as the front door
opened.

Quinn.

"Hi," she called out, rushing to the front door. Her stomach fluttered at the sight of Quinn in his jeans and damp, fitted white T-shirt. As she walked toward him though, she noticed how tired he looked. It was eight o'clock at night, for crying out loud, and she knew his day must have been grueling.

"Hey, Holly," he said, taking off his boots, barely looking at her as he followed her through the house, work boots in hand.

"Where's the problem?" he asked.

"Huge flood in the basement," she said, biting her lip.

He threw his head back briefly and groaned, then marched on past her, bounding down the old stairs two at a time. She watched silently as he stopped on the bottom step and yanked on his boots before trudging through the water. She stopped hesitantly halfway down the stairs.

"What are you doing?" she called out, feeling bad that she wasn't helping.

"Looking for the source of the flooding." His back was still to her as he looked around the basement.

"Oh," she said, feeling completely useless. "Can I help?"

"Don't worry about it." He waded across the basement floor and examined a window.

Holly held her breath. *Please don't let it be the windows, please don't let it be the windows…*

Quinn cursed and then hoisted himself up to look at the small window. "Here it is," he mumbled as he did something to the glass.

She couldn't quite see what he was doing. She was busy trying to fight the rush of desire she felt at the sight of his muscles straining against his T-shirt as he hoisted himself up onto the window ledge. Clearly, she had been spending too much time in the city, where men were covered up in slick suits and didn't spend all day working with their hands, using their muscles…

"Holly, you listening?" He looked irritated, judging by his formidable stance in the middle of the room.

"Sorry, I didn't catch that last bit," Holly stammered, tearing her eyes away from the long, lean lines of his jeans.

Quinn shook his head and walked toward her. "I said, I've got to get outside and see what I can do to keep the water from seeping through those windows."

He walked back to the stairs, and Holly held her breath. He paused abruptly on his way up the steps and pulled his wet boots off. "Didn't the window guys say they'd install the windows this week?" he asked, his eyes narrowing in on her.

She didn't say anything. *Uh-oh.*

He raised his eyebrows. "Well?"

She looked at Quinn's thunderous expression, his wet jeans and shirt, and thought this might not be the best time to test the man's patience. "I believe in order for them to install the windows, I would have actually had to order them," she said, biting her lip. She watched the veins in his neck stand at attention. One of them sort of looked like it might snap free like a violin string. He shut his eyes for a moment, then stalked past her toward the back door. She could swear she heard him grumble something about designers. "It was a tough call to make. I thought I made the right decision. And, um, I've got the Realtor coming over tomorrow, and I just—"

"What?" he said, standing with his hand on the doorknob. Those veins in his neck looked ready to pop again.

"You know, the Realtor, to list the house? I'd hate for her to see the basement all flooded."

Quinn opened his mouth, looked at her a second longer, and then shut it. He whipped open the back door and a gust of wind tore through the room.

"Quinn, put a jacket on at least!"

He slammed the door shut against the wind. "It was a stupid move, Holly. Your decision to have quartzite counter-tops over new basement windows just cost you a couple of grand in water damage," he said, pulling on his boots.

"Well, a prospective buyer would be more likely to look at a kitchen closely than at a basement," she said, her words trailing off ever so slightly when it looked like his head was about to pop off his neck.

He was a force to be reckoned with when he was angry, all hard lines and hot masculine energy. Hot, masculine energy. *What was wrong with her?*

"Really? Well, if *I* were buying a house, the first place I'd look is the basement," he said, "especially if I knew some hot-shot designer had done the reno to make a quick buck." And with those lovely parting words, he stormed outside.

Ouch. How was she supposed to know this would happen? And there was no way flooding in an unfinished base-ment would cost that much.

She did feel bad, though. Quinn had been here every day, going over and above for her. She knew he was tired and worn out, and now she had added to it. Between her place and his other responsibilities, he'd been pushing too hard. She walked to the French doors and peered through the glass. The rain was coming down sideways in the strong wind. The remaining fall leaves had been completely stripped from the trees and flew around the yard angrily.

Quinn was going to be soaked. And mad. She hovered, occasionally peeking out the window for any sign of him.

Coffee. He would want coffee. She heard banging and cursing below the kitchen window as she brewed a pot.

Towels. She should get him some towels. She ran upstairs and took a couple of large, fluffy white towels from the newly staged linen closet in the hallway.

She paused on the second step from the bottom of the staircase as Quinn walked in, sopping wet, and pulled off his boots on the front rug.

He looked angry. And very, very delicious. She really shouldn't be relishing in the sight of him. After all, he must be freezing in those wet clothes that were clinging to the powerful lines of his tall, strong body.

She was so going to Hell.

"Are you going to hand me one of those towels, or just tease me with the sight of them?" he snapped. Quinn rarely lost his cool. Right now, he was looking very, very close to losing it.

She pursed her lips with disapproval but walked over and handed him a towel.

"Thanks," he grumbled as he toweled off his hair.

"Sorry, Quinn," she said reluctantly. She wasn't sorry about the quartzite counters, but she did feel bad that he had to deal with her mistake. He stopped drying his hair and looked into her eyes, the silence between them deafening as the wind and rain recklessly beat against the windows and roof.

"Holly, do you know what I want to do right now?"

Holly swallowed. Hard. "Take a hot bath?"

He shook his head and took a step closer.

She could barely breathe. "A hot shower?"

He shook his head again and his eyes dropped to her mouth. Her lips parted involuntarily.

"Coffee?" she managed to whisper as she heard the beep signaling the brew cycle had finished. He shook his head again and stood a few inches away from her.

"I want to kiss you," he said, his voice deep, and then he gently took her wrist and tugged her toward him. "I want to kiss you and taste you and never stop."

Holly felt her knees wobble as her eyes went from his to his lips. "I really don't taste that good, Quinn," she whispered, all the while staring at his mouth.

"Oh, yeah, I bet you do," he said. Panic and desire intertwined throughout her body. Could she do this? Could she do this and survive? Would she still be able to leave and move on?

His hand went to her waist, and she jumped at the feel of his hand on her body, hot and real and alive. Ten years of wanting, of waiting, had culminated into this very moment. And now that it was here, that he was here, she was the one turning into the chicken.

"I have a feeling you're going to taste better than all the fantasies I've had about you," he murmured in a low, throaty voice that was as much a turn on as the words he spoke.

"Fantasies?" she whispered, her breath shallow. Her eyes moved from his intense blue gaze to his sensual, chiseled lips so close to hers. She took in the rugged plains of his handsome face and knew that, yes, she could do this. This was Quinn.

She wanted to feel the man that had filled her memories

and dreams for the last ten years. She wanted to know what his skin felt like, tasted like. She wanted to know the feel of his mouth on hers. She wanted to know what it would be like to have her body pressed against his, skin against skin. Her hands climbed the taught, warm muscles of his arms, and she walked into the embrace that had been waiting for her for ten long years. It was as though she was finally coming home to the only man who'd ever been able to reach her heart and soul.

"Oh, yeah, real hot fantasies. And I think you need to know how I really wanted to kiss you that last night," he whispered. And then his mouth was on hers. Consuming, demanding, and so perfectly Quinn that she melted into the hard planes of his body and relinquished all thought. His mouth moved over hers again and again, until all her breath was gone. When she drew his tongue into her mouth, he captured the gasp that tore from her throat, and then she was plastered against the wet wall of his chest. Holly whimpered and felt her knees give as his hands roamed her body, each place he touched making her need him more.

· · ·

"God, I think I've wanted you forever," Quinn rasped against her lips. He couldn't move away from her, not even for a second. But he needed to know that she was ready for this. There was a vulnerability about Holly that made him want to be certain that she was comfortable moving their relationship forward. She had been through so much, and he'd rather die than add to her sadness. He didn't want any regrets tomorrow morning—for either of them.

A Risk Worth Taking

Her eyes, greener than he'd ever seen them and spar-kling with life, with desire, dropped to his lips. "Me, too," she whispered, and for a second he could have sworn he saw something flash across her eyes. But it was gone before he was sure. Quinn leaned down to pick her up, finding himself filled with the need to make love to her until she forgot all the pain, and surrendered only to the pleasure.

"Don't drop me," she said with a kiss against his bare throat, and he felt her smile as he carried her up the stairs.

"I'd never drop you," he answered.

"Well, you did, remember—"

Quinn was laughing when he bent his head and halted the words from leaving her soft mouth.

"You fell. That wasn't my fault," he said as he reached the bedroom. The fireplace was already lit and casting an inviting glow in the otherwise shadowed room. He slowly set her down so they were both standing in front of the fire-place. He didn't take his hands from her as he circled her waist. He couldn't let go, ever again. She was the one he couldn't forget, and now she was here. And their age dif-ference no longer mattered. This was the night that would change everything between them…forever.

Her face was flushed, her eyes brilliant, reflecting her desire. "Well, you still could have caught me." She smiled, her hands, soft and light, slowly climbing his forearms until they settled around his neck.

"I told you I'd hang the damn chandelier," he murmured, finding it increasingly difficult to have a conversation. The overwhelming urge to have his mouth on her body won out and he leaned down to kiss her neck. When she sighed against him, his lips traveled the length of her impossibly soft and fragrant neck until he reached her earlobe. He took the gentle flesh between his teeth and caught Holly as she sank into him.

"Quinn," she said in a husky voice before tugging the front of his shirt and pulling him lower for a kiss. She lifted his T-shirt over his head and dropped it to the ground. She pulled back to look at him, her lips parted, and he had never felt so aroused by a woman's stare. Her hands clutched his waist and then roamed up his torso and his chest, and all he could do was clench his teeth at the excruciating torment. He felt her lips slowly open over his hot skin as she planted featherlike kisses across his chest, and her hands moved to the top button of his jeans. Sweet torture. But enough was enough. He wanted Holly naked and hot with him. He wanted to feel her bare skin against his, and then he wanted to be inside of her.

He felt her breasts graze against his chest and he groaned from deep in his throat. "God, I want to see you, and taste you, and kiss you." He drew her shirt over her head and she stood in front of him in the sexiest lace bra. It wasn't the bra he realized a half second later, it was the woman. He traced his tongue along her collarbone and felt her knees buckle as his mouth closed over the nipple that was begging for his attention through the transparent lace. He caught her against him, and he dragged them both to the bed. Quinn covered her body with his, his lips exploring her skin, his hands moving to cup her breasts. She filled his hands, and then his lips replaced his hand as he took her nipple in his mouth, groaning against her as she arched under him and helped shrug off her jeans.

"Quinn," she said in a voice that sent off a few warning

bells, even in his state of all-out arousal.

"Yeah," he said, on his way to remove the last piece of lace covering her with his teeth.

"Nevermind," she moaned as he reached his destination, her hands now on his head, clutching his hair between her fingers.

"Just hurry up and tell me—whatever it is," he said, lowering her panties on the sweet journey down her long, silky legs.

"There was just something I thought I should mention," she whispered, drawing him back up to her. Her eyes were on him, and her hands were on the front of his jeans.

"Tell me," he ground out as she cupped him through his jeans. He squeezed his eyes shut, balancing himself on his forearms, and prayed she would hurry up with whatever it was that she thought was so dire.

"Do you remember when I said I'd wait for you?" she whispered, her green eyes locking onto his, her hands slowly starting to unbutton his jeans. He bit down hard on his back teeth.

He gave a short nod, trying to concentrate on her words. But now her breasts were pressed against him, and her hands began stroking him.

"Right. Well, I just thought it might be a good time to tell you that I did."

Everything in Quinn's body came to a grinding halt. What the hell was she talking about? God, not that. It all stopped for one painful moment, before blood came roaring to his ears and he found his voice. He shook his head. "No. No, you didn't," he whispered.

She nodded, staring straight through him in that way

only she could. "Yeah, uh-huh, I did," and then she slid her hands down his pants.

He swore out loud.

"I waited. For this. For you," she whispered, reaching up to kiss him again.

Quinn's mind whirled. "What about that ugly Daniel guy Claire told me about?" he rasped against her lips, trying to form coherent thoughts, trying to wrap his head around this.

She pressed her head into the pillow and frowned at him. "Claire said what? Daniel isn't ugly—"

"What about—"

"I never thought you'd be such a talker in bed, Quinn."

Quinn opened his mouth, about to remedy her impression of him, but Holly continued speaking.

"His hands weren't your hands, and, God, I just wanted your hands on me, Quinn."

Quinn stared at her, their bodies still pressed together, and he couldn't find the words for the emotion coursing through his body.

Every single ounce of self-control he'd been desperately holding on to was obliterated. He locked his eyes with hers as he pulled Holly's hands from his body, holding them above her head on the pillow. He bent his head and showed her with his mouth, with his body, what she meant to him. He wanted to make up for the years they'd been apart, for the years they'd gone without loving each other. As he worshiped her body, her words echoed in his mind. As she whimpered beneath him, as she clutched his head, tugging at his hair, as her nails dug into his skin, and as he entered her, he knew that no matter what happened, this woman would always claim a piece of him.

Chapter Eight

Quinn lay on his back, staring at the ceiling.

His hands weren't your hands… How on earth did she expect that he'd hear her say these things and be able to just say good-bye in a few weeks? He couldn't. He knew what that meant, even if she didn't want to admit it. She'd waited for him, just as she'd said that night ten years ago. It humbled him. And it made him never want to be without her again.

What the hell were they going to do now? Somehow, someway, Holly always managed to complicate things. Two hours ago, was he even thinking that he'd be in this bed, after having what had to be the most profound, intense sexual experience of his entire life? No. And a few nights ago, when Holly was calling him a chicken, did he even entertain that the hot-as-hell woman had actually kept her promise and "waited" for him?

What were their options? He'd offered her a job and she'd refused. She was scared to live here again. How could he argue that? He hadn't lived through what she had, couldn't fully understand her fears. But he also knew that she was living in denial if she thought that running back to her old life could make the memories disappear.

He had his own demons, his own guilt. But if working through them meant having Holly in his life, then he'd do it. He was going to see Christine. He needed to fully atone for what he did and how he failed her. He had tried once, but it had been too soon, and the wounds had been too fresh for both of them. And despite the fact that he and Christine would never have worked, and they never should have been together in the first place, he needed to apologize. He needed to, in order to move on.

Holly was going to push him away. He knew that. Or she was going to try, anyway. She put on this brave front, but she was probably the most vulnerable woman he'd ever met. And she didn't deal with her feelings. Hell, not that he was an expert, but the amount of emotion that Holly was holding on to inside—the amount that she thought she had control over—was going to come to the surface one way or another. And he was determined to be the man she needed him to be when those emotions finally surfaced. He listened to her deep, even breathing as she slept curled against him, while the rain pattered against the windows, and he wished that they could stay here forever.

• • •

She was warm, and she was safe, and everything was as it should be.

Hard, firm flesh beneath her fingertips and the increasing

rhythm of her heart told her Quinn was still beside her — or half under her. Her head was on his chest, and her leg was wrapped around his. And there wasn't any place in the world she'd rather be. She could fool herself for the rest of the night that this could last. Why did she need to think of all the reasons this was wrong? Why couldn't she live in the moment, just this once?

"Welcome back, Holly," Quinn said, the smile in his voice obvious, the words achingly familiar. *Quinn.* Exquisite memories wafted over her like a billowing silk scarf. Much better than any dream. She slowly lifted her head and looked into the face she adored.

"Hi," she said, smiling at him. He was magnificent to look at. His hair was mussed, and a five o'clock shadow outlined the strong lines of his face. There was warmth in his eyes that was so disarming, and so genuine, that it nearly brought tears to her eyes.

"Feels like I've been waiting forever to make love to you," Quinn said gruffly, a gentle smile teasing his lips as he smoothed the tangled hair off her shoulders.

"You were worth waiting for," Holly whispered as her eyes traced his features, and inevitably trailed down his bare flesh. She felt desire begin to bubble again. No man she'd ever dated had that effect on her. And it occurred to her that this was the first time since Jennifer and Rick had died that she felt peace. And truly happy.

"If you keep looking at me like that, Holly, I don't think we'll make it out of this bed until next week," Quinn said, one hand grazing her spine.

"If only that were an option," she murmured, resting her chin on his chest.

"I can't think of any other thing I'd rather do for the entire week than stay right here. Speaking of which, where's Ella?"

"She's with Claire for the night," Holly said, as his eyes reflected her thoughts.

"So, we've got the whole night."

"Yup, and I think we need wine," she said with a sly smile.

"And food. Do you have anything to eat in that kitchen?"

"I spent it all on the counters," she teased.

"Cute. Very cute," he said, smiling as he kissed her.

"I have about six jars of organic baby food and a giant bag of kettle chips," she said sheepishly. She had planned on devouring that bag in lieu of dinner and in dedication to her sorry life. "Groceries were the last item on my to-do list, but then you showed up, and look what's happened."

"Yeah, a real shame." He laughed. "Fine, you like Chinese food?"

Holly nodded. Really, she couldn't care less what they ate.

"Okay, I'll order," he said, sitting up. He reached for his jeans and pulled his cell phone from the pocket. Holly contentedly watched as he ordered enough for ten people.

"You keep the Chinese restaurant on speed dial?" she asked, smiling.

He grinned. "I don't have time to cook," he said, falling back on the pillows and tugging her along with him. "So let's talk."

"About what?" Dread hummed through her. "We don't need to talk about anything," she said, drumming her fingers against his chest. She couldn't stop touching him.

The corner of Quinn's mouth lifted. "Funny, because a few hours ago, when your hands were down my pants, you couldn't seem to stop talking—"

Holly swallowed the nervous laugh in her throat and pursed her lips. "That is crass."

"Not crass. Honest," he said with one of those disarming smiles.

"Well, that was then and this is now. And really, now that everything is out in the open, what more could there possibly be to discuss?" she asked, her voice trailing off as he rolled his eyes.

"Haven't you figured out yet that your clever little attempts at getting out of honest conversation only make me more intent on figuring you out?"

"I thought men hated talking. Isn't it me who's supposed to want the heartfelt discussion?"

"Yeah, normally the last thing I'd want to do is have a heart-to-heart. But nothing about us is normal," Quinn said, his eyes not leaving her face.

"Fine. I figured you might…have a *few* questions," she said hesitantly as she touched the hairs on Quinn's chest.

"Can you stop doing that?" Quinn asked when she accidentally pulled at one.

"Sorry, I thought it was gray," she said, barely holding onto her smile.

He laughed and then kissed her. "Nice try."

"There is nothing to tell. Really. I just never met anyone that interested me. I've been busy. Now that I'm back here and have time off work—"

Quinn's laugh and the rumbling of his chest under her chin made her stop speaking to glare at him—or try to glare at him, anyway. He kissed her, long and hard, and then ruined that when he began laughing against her lips.

"What's so funny?"

"You're such a liar. You expect me to believe that the only reason we're in this bed is because you happened to have some spare time?"

Holly nodded. She couldn't look him in the eye though, so she concentrated on looking at his eyebrows. "You don't have to make it sound absurd."

"It *is* absurd—and a pile of bull. We are here because this is what we've both wanted for a long, long time. And correct me if I'm wrong, but while you happened to be naked under me, I believe you where whispering something about my hands."

"It was just an expression."

"Funny, I'm not familiar with that one."

"And it's actually quite rude for you to bring up random things we said while we were in bed together."

"Well, you can bring up anything I said and repeat it to me now if you'd like. I stand by whatever I said while I was taking off your clothes or inside—"

"No need to repeat anything. And I didn't say anything, anyways," Holly said in a shrill voice as the recollection of the words he'd whispered infused her with a searing heat. Quinn was very talented in expressing his thoughts, she'd learned.

He tapped his finger on his chin. "Well, I'm pretty sure I heard the words faster and hard—"

"That's very arrogant of you."

"No, Holl, if I were arrogant, would I actually admit that *you*, who had never done any of this before, were giving *me*

instructions—"

"They weren't *instructions*."

"They were *explicit* instructions. And it was very hot," he said in a low voice and with a grin that was far too smug. She found herself smiling with him, his warm skin beneath her hands more perfect to her than she had ever dreamed. Yet fear began teasing her. It sneaked into her psyche, making everything a little less bright, a little less rosy. Holly felt her smile quiver ever so slightly, trying to believe, trying to be brave.

"What's wrong?" Quinn asked, smoothing her hair gently. Holly fought against the surge of emotion that his tenderness brought on. She wanted to tell him everything, she wanted to lean on him and rely on him.

"Will you stay?" Holly whispered, not caring that he saw her vulnerability.

He frowned. "Of course I'll stay. Where would I go?" he said roughly. Holly didn't answer him. She didn't want to say that eventually everyone leaves, or tell him that she wanted to stay here forever—that he made her feel safe, and loved, and for the first time, truly whole.

"Need help opening that bottle of wine?" Holly teased as Quinn struggled with the cork.

"If you open bottles of wine like you hang chandeliers, then no thanks," Quinn said, laughing as she pinched his waist.

"That's so rude." Holly laughed, admiring how good he looked standing there in his jeans and sweater. He finally uncorked the bottle and poured them each a glass. Quinn had spent the entire day with Holly and Ella. They had gotten off to a rocky start when Sabrina, the Realtor, had come over bright and early to do a thorough appraisal of the home. Sabrina had been impressed, and they'd agreed on a price that was even more than Holly had hoped for. The house would be ready to be put on the market the same day as the party. Holly had braced herself for Quinn's reaction, but he'd been silent most of the time, and when she'd signed the listing papers, he had left the room.

As Holly was signing her name on the agreement, she'd had to forcibly push aside the thoughts of her grandparents and Jennifer. She couldn't allow herself to feel guilt. They weren't here. She was the one left standing, holding all the baggage. She knew they'd understand her need to protect herself. The money from the sale would ensure Ella's future. Selling the house was something she had to do, regardless of what Quinn thought.

Quinn had spent the night, and then the day. They had picked up Ella soon after Sabrina left and then gone for brunch. After, they'd enjoyed a long, fun Sunday afternoon, just the three of them. It was how she imagined a real family would spend time together. They went out for groceries, came home, played with Ella, gave her a bath, and had put her to bed. Now they were about to sit down to dinner.

"So, are we going to talk about you putting this place up for sale, or are we going to pretend that you're not leaving soon?" Quinn asked, changing the mood from fun to tense in one second flat. Holly's mouth went dry as she stared across the island to him. She knew this would happen. There was too much unresolved between them.

A muffled sound broke through the silence of the kitchen. Holly sat up straight on the bar stool, on guard. "Did you hear that?" Holly asked.

Quinn frowned, nodding.

It had sounded like Ella. But it wasn't a cry. Holly immediately thought of Ella's runny nose that had started earlier in the day, but she hadn't worried too much about it.

"Let's go check on her," Quinn said, taking her hand as they tiptoed up the stairs and slowly opened the door to Ella's room. Ella was sitting up in her crib, and even with only the dim glow of the nightlight, Holly could see how red her face was.

"Hi, sweetheart," Holly whispered, rushing over to pick her up while trying to fight the rising panic that threatened to consume her. Ella whimpered and held out her arms. Her skin was on fire, scorching Holly's hands through the fuzzy sleeper.

"She's boiling," Holly gasped as she sat her on the changing table.

Quinn placed his hand on Ella's cheeks and forehead and frowned. "She is really hot," he agreed, the worry in his face and voice intensifying Holly's own. Ella's pink face scrunched up, and Quinn tried to soothe her by rubbing her back and talking to her.

Dread slithered through Holly's body, insidious and debilitating, as she looked at Ella and tried to form a coherent thought.

"Do you have a thermometer?" Quinn asked.

Holly nodded. "Thermometer," she murmured. She crossed the room to the closet where she had stashed a box filled with baby supplies. She needed to focus, she needed to remain calm and in control. But the moment she crossed the room, Ella started crying and coughing, a rough, barky cough that Holly knew was no ordinary cold. Holly went still, her fear making her limbs useless and heavy.

"Come here, baby," she heard Quinn whisper as he picked Ella up. Quinn knew exactly what to do. And he was calm.

With shaking hands, Holly yanked down the box from the upper shelf of the closet, pulled out the thermometer, and crossed the room. Quinn was holding Ella and rubbing her back, his mouth set in a straight line.

"I don't like the sound of that cough," Quinn said as Holly pried open the blue thermometer case, willing her hands not to shake. She had never used the baby thermometer before, the instructions still neatly tucked inside the case. She unfolded the paper, taking deep breaths, telling herself to concentrate. Ella was going to be fine. Just check her temperature. Hurry up. How hard was it to grasp the simple directions? But it was hard when all she could think about was going to the hospital, of Ella not getting better, of—

"Here, you hold Ella, and I'll get this thing going," Quinn suggested gently. Holly nodded, looking into his eyes as he handed Ella over. He knew.

A few moments later, Quinn pressed a button that lit up the digital screen. Ella was still wheezing as Quinn gently positioned the thermometer in her ear, just as the diagram on the instruction manual indicated. "One hundred and two," he said, putting the thermometer back in the case. Holly nodded. What should she do? Her mind was hurling around thoughts that were premature and devastating. She rubbed her sweaty hands down the front of her jeans, trying

to focus.

"Why don't we take this pajama thing off of her? She's too hot," Quinn said, already unzipping the sleeper. Holly nodded numbly, looking at Ella's flushed skin and glassy eyes. At least she hadn't made that horrible coughing noise again. "Do you have baby Tylenol or something?" Quinn asked as he gently smoothed Ella's sweaty hair off her forehead.

Holly nodded automatically. *Acetaminophen.* Of course, that would help with the fever. She crossed the room again and pulled the brand-new bottle out of the box. Quinn had Ella in his arms and was gently patting her bare back as she rested against him with just her diaper on. Holly held the bottle in her hand and tried to focus on the dosing. But her eyes blurred with tears and her hand shook. She knew Quinn was watching her. She was going to do this. *What kind of idiot can't figure out the dose on a bottle of Tylenol?* She blinked rapidly. Quinn placed Ella back on the changing table and then gently pried the bottle from Holly's hands. He dosed it and softly squeezed the liquid into Ella's mouth. Holly watched, helplessly. She was a coward, she was useless—and Quinn was nice enough not to mention it.

Quinn pulled his cell phone out of his pocket. "I'm going to give Evan a call, okay? I know he's at Jake's place tonight."

As Quinn spoke to Evan, Holly tried to look calm for Ella's sake. But just knowing that Quinn thought they needed a doctor made everything more serious.

"Do you think she has something horrible?" Holly asked the second he hung up the phone.

"Babies and kids get sick all the time. She's going to be fine. I promise, Holly. She's going to be fine," Quinn said harshly, leaning out with one hand to touch her cheek. Tears pricked her eyes immediately.

"Why don't we go wait downstairs," Quinn suggested, reaching out for her hand, while carrying Ella. Holly nodded and clutched his hand, grateful for his strength. They stood in the darkened living room, staring out the bay window, waiting for Evan. Just as Ella started coughing again, headlights appeared down the dark road and his car pulled into the driveway. Evan ran up the steps as Holly opened the front door.

"Hi guys," Evan said, shrugging out of his coat and stepping into the house, his doctor's bag in hand.

"Thanks for coming so quickly," Holly said, taking his coat as Ella started crying and coughing again. Holly wrapped her arms around herself and stood still, not walking into the living room. Quinn was rocking Ella and Holly could hear him whispering to her softly. She stood on the sidelines as Evan approached Ella and greeted her. Both brothers stood with Ella between them, their size and strength in blatant contrast to the gentleness with which they treated little Ella. Holly fought the tears threatening to overflow.

"Let me just have a look at her and ask you some questions, okay?" Evan said, turning around to look at Holly.

Holly nodded and stepped closer.

"Sure," Quinn answered, handing Ella over to him. He turned to look at Holly, and the second he made eye contact, his face softened and he walked over to her. She couldn't fake being okay. It was too much. Ella kept coughing and crying as Evan listened to her breathing. Holly felt Quinn grab her hand in his and squeeze it as Evan continued his examination.

"She has croup, Holly."

"Croup? Where would she have picked that up?"

"It's about as contagious as the common cold. It can become very serious, but I wouldn't worry about that at this point."

Holly felt tears prick the back of her eyes as she nodded.

"Let's go upstairs, run the hot water in the shower, and close the door to the washroom," Evan said. "The moist air will help. I'll stay until she's doing better and you're comfortable." Ella started coughing again, and Holly read the concern on Evan's face. He asked her a few questions about Ella's health in general as they made their way upstairs. Holly answered as best she could. Quinn immediately ran the hot water when they entered the bathroom and Evan shut the door.

Evan gave Holly a smile. "She's going to be fine, Holly. The best way to treat it at this point is to keep Ella calm and happy. The humidity and moisture from the steam will help open up her breathing passages. Croup is a viral infection that is pretty common for children under five. It causes swelling in the vocal cords, which is what is giving her that raspy, barky cough. But you did everything right, Holly, giving her some acetaminophen—that's helping with the fever."

Holly listened while rocking Ella and giving her little reassuring kisses. But she hadn't thought about the acetaminophen—that had been Quinn. She had been paralyzed. She had done nothing. She hadn't even been able to take her temperature.

Quinn walked over. "Why don't I hold her for a bit?"

Holly nodded and handed Ella to him. Ella immediately rested her head on his shoulder. Intense emotion bubbled inside Holly's chest before it coursed through her body as she watched Quinn hold Ella so tenderly. She couldn't lose Ella.

The realization that Ella wasn't just a niece, a baby to care for, gripped her, and drowned her in fear and love. Ella encompassed her very soul. Something had happened. Somehow, Ella had cut through Holly's defenses and become the light of her life. Her smile, her face, her laugh. She couldn't imagine life without her.

Or without the man holding her.

After about twenty minutes, Ella's coughing became more sporadic, until she finally was breathing comfortably in Quinn's arms. Evan checked her temperature again and was pleased by the results.

"If you have to go, Evan, you can. Just tell us what we should do if it gets worse," Quinn whispered.

"Okay. I've got to be back at the hospital in an hour, so I'm going to leave soon. But if she can lie down after an hour or so and get back to sleep that's a very good sign. I'd suggest you sleep in her room tonight just to be sure. If you see her breathing becomes more labored and it looks as though she's having trouble drawing in a breath, drooling excessively, looks really pale, take her into the ER, okay?"

Trouble breathing. ER. Holly never wanted to go to that place again. Her stomach felt tight and nausea circled around her.

"But she's going to be fine, Ev, right? Tell Holly she's going to be okay." Quinn's eyes darted from Evan to Holly.

Evan nodded quickly. "Yes. Holly, she's going to be fine," Evan said, reaching out to touch her shoulder. Holly nodded numbly. They didn't know. No one knew. One minute people

were fine and the next they were a memory.

"She's a tough cookie, I can tell. And she's already responding to the humidity in here." Holly looked over at Ella, who did look better. Her head was on Quinn's chest and she was breathing peacefully.

"Thank you," Holly whispered to Evan.

"Anytime. Tomorrow, you should go buy a humidifier for her room. Maybe sleep with the window open just an inch or two in her room tonight to let in some moisture. Just make sure she's warm enough."

"Thanks, Ev," Quinn said with a nod to his brother.

"No problem. I'm glad you called me." Evan washed his hands in the sink and then rolled down his sleeves. "Okay, baby, have a good sleep," Evan said, ruffling Ella's hair.

"I'll see you out, Evan," Holly whispered.

Holly and Evan walked down the stairs side by side, neither of them saying anything.

Evan stopped at the front door and turned to her. "She'll be fine, Holly."

Holly forced a smile. "I know. Thank you."

He nodded, and then turned to get his jacket. She thought he was going to leave, but he suddenly stopped and turned around. His expression was intense, intimidating almost. "I wouldn't be where I am today if it wasn't for Quinn. I'd do anything for him. He's the best man I've ever known, Holly."

Holly stared at Evan's handsome features, stared into the blue eyes that were so similar to Quinn's, and nodded. She knew what he meant. She knew it down to her bones. Quinn was a man who didn't hide from his problems. He was not the type to run. She managed a brief smile. "I know.

Thank you again, Evan."

He nodded, putting on his coat. "You're welcome. Don't hesitate to call me if her condition changes or if you have any questions, okay?" He waited for her nod, then opened the door and walked out. Holly carefully shut the door behind him and locked it. She could hear the sound of Quinn's low voice coming from upstairs. Tears burned the back of her eyes, and she turned off lights as she walked upstairs with weary legs.

The soft glow from the light in the master bedroom told Holly where they were. She walked in to find Quinn slowly pacing the room, Ella sleeping against his shoulder. Quinn smiled, and everything inside of Holly melted. The sight of him, tall and strong and powerful, with her angelic niece drooling on his shirt, was the most beautiful thing she'd ever seen.

It was the most beautiful and the most terrifying. Quinn was in this room, in the house that held so many memories, with the little girl that had become the world to her. If anyone saw them, they would think they were a family. And that was what was so frightening. Because with each day that passed, she wanted them to be one. So badly. Quinn had walked her through a nightmare and been her rock. When she thought she was going to panic, he'd held on and guided her out of it. She had fallen back on him. And he'd been there. But she'd be foolish if she thought it could always be that way. Life had a way of snatching people away and robbing you of your safety.

"How about she sleeps with us tonight," Quinn whispered from across the room. *Us.* They were all here together, and that's what a family would do. That's what Jennifer and Rick would have done. Holly's eyes filled with tears at the thought of her sister and brother-in-law. She wrapped her arms around herself, fighting her need to stay alone and removed, yet wanting the comfort of feeling loved and together. She nodded rapidly, determined not to break down. Not now.

"Thank you. I don't know what would have happened—"

"You would have been fine."

Holly shook her head, not able to argue. "I'm so tired. I feel like I haven't slept in almost a year," she whispered raggedly, trying not to cry.

"Holly," he whispered, crossing the room in two strides. "She's fine. Everything is going be okay. Go put on your penguin pajamas and get ready for bed. No room for arguing," he ordered in an impossibly gentle voice, tilting his head toward the washroom door. He pressed a kiss on the top of her head and leaned back to look at her. Holly's chin wobbled, because the concern in his eyes and the tenderness in his voice told her everything she needed to know. For the first time in her life, she was ready to relinquish control. She nodded and crossed the room.

Five minutes later, after changing into her pajamas, brushing her teeth, and removing whatever was left of her makeup, she emerged from the washroom. Quinn was standing by the fireplace, Ella still sleeping soundly in his arms.

Holly walked toward the bed, and her heart squeezed as she saw that he had turned down the duvet and plumped her pillows. A glass of fresh water was sitting on the nightstand as well. She climbed into bed, and he drew the covers over her with one arm. He crossed to the other side of the bed and gingerly sat next to her with his back propped up against the headboard and Ella resting on his chest.

"Go to sleep. The world will go on without you for a few hours. Everything will be fine," he said, giving her a reassuring smile. Holly nodded, her eyes focused on the picture Quinn and Ella made together. She felt peace wash over her as she huddled further under the duvet, and when she fell asleep a few seconds later, she had a soft smile on her face.

Chapter Nine

Holly opened her eyes slowly, feeling an intense pressure against her chest. It was hard to breathe. As her eyes focused on Quinn, who was sound asleep with Ella snoring on top of him, Holly knew the source of her pain. She tried to take a deep breath as she stared at the two of them. They looked like father and daughter — and maybe in another world, they could be. She could be a wife and a mother. But all of that entailed the promise of safety, of a happy ending. But Holly knew that no one could ever make her that promise. No one could tell her that everything would be okay, and that she and Quinn would grow old together. That Ella would grow up and be happy and healthy.

Everything that had happened in the last twenty-four hours had been laced with the bittersweet warning against loving too deeply. She knew how this would end, even if Quinn didn't. Which was why she needed to go back to Toronto.

Quinn's eyes opened slowly, and Holly held her breath. Her heart constricted painfully as his hand immediately went to smooth Ella's hair. And then his eyes landed on hers, filled with the emotion that she wanted to run from. He was the man that she could never forget—hard and strong, combined with that mix of tenderness that only he could pull off so well. He made her want to give up her solitary existence, abandon her career in Toronto. He made her want to believe that people stayed, that people lived, that love could conquer everything.

"Morning," he whispered, his voice deliciously low and smooth.

"Morning," Holly answered, pulling the duvet up and tucking it under her chin.

"She slept through the rest of the night," Quinn said over Ella's gentle snoring.

Holly nodded. "She doesn't even look like she has a fever anymore," she whispered.

"Didn't I tell you everything would be okay?"

Holly bit down on her tongue until it hurt.

"Holly?" Quinn said, frowning when she didn't answer.

"You're right." She nodded.

"Why do you look like you're about to cry?" he asked, reaching out to smooth her hair off her face.

Holly felt the sting of tears as she looked into his eyes. She *was* about to cry.

"You know what, why don't I put Ella in her crib and then come back, okay?" he asked, carefully rising from the bed. He walked out of the room, not waiting for her reply. And before Holly had a chance to panic, he was back.

"She actually went to sleep?" Holly asked.

He nodded. "Poor thing is wiped," he said, joining her in bed. "And I think you are, too." He lifted her hand to his lips, his touch offering her safety, beckoning her honesty. Holly traced the hard line of his shoulder, his strength, his heat, reminding her that he was real, that Quinn was here.

"What are you so afraid of, Holly?"

"Everything," she answered.

Quinn frowned slightly, shifting so that he propped himself on his elbow, his hand still locked with hers. "Tell me," he said softly, but with enough force in his voice that Holly knew he wasn't going to let it drop. She turned to him, not wanting to hide, wanting to confide in the man that had always made her feel safe.

"I can't do this."

"What?"

"This," she whispered, waving her hands between them. "This pretend family thing."

"It doesn't have to be pretend," he said, brushing her hair off her shoulder. Holly fought the urge to pull away from him, to get out of the bed and put as much distance between them as possible.

"I'm not her mother. I can't pretend to be."

"Whoa," he said harshly. "You *are* her mother now. What happened was horrible. But you are here and Ella is here—"

"I'm not a parent," Holly said, clenching her hands into fists around the sheet.

"You are."

She shook her head rapidly. "No. No. I'm not a mom. I will never be. I'm nothing like Jennifer," she said, pausing to suck in some air. "I cut her. That first week, I had to clip Ella's nails and I cut the skin," she gushed, a hiccup escaping her lips. "Look what happened last night. I was useless. I have no idea what I'm doing. I don't know how to be a mom. What happens when she goes to school and it's Mother's Day and they make those little cards for their moms? What if she hates me, what if she tells me—"

"Did you hate your grandmother?"

Holly stared past him, looking at the fireplace. He didn't get it. "Of course not."

"And when you were in school and it was Mother's Day, did you make a card for your grandmother instead?"

Holly nodded, feeling tears begin to tease the back of her eyes and deep in her throat.

"She's going to love you. No, she already loves you, and one day when she's old enough to understand, you'll show her pictures of Jen and Rick, and you'll tell her how much they loved her. But you are her family now. You've done everything for Ella. And she loves you. And when she's old enough and you tell her about Jen and Rick, she's still going to love you. You're not Jen, you're you. And she will always love you. Holly," he said, looking into her eyes, "stay here. Stay here and give us a chance."

"I can't do that," she said, shaking her head and trying to get up. His hand clamped down on her wrist just hard enough that she knew he meant business. His jaw was clenched and his eyes glittered. "Stop running away," he said harshly.

Holly held his gaze, not backing down an inch. She was running. She knew she was. But it was her choice. She was the one who had to figure out how to survive. He couldn't do it for her. She yanked her arm free of his grasp, the air cool on the skin that was once warmed by his touch.

"I can't stay here. I have a job to get back to. I have a

home in Toronto, a job, a life. This is not my house—"

"How can you believe that? Of course this is your house."

Holly shook her head. "I already explained this to you. It was supposed to be Jen and Rick's. They should be here, not me."

Quinn just stared at her, his expression impassive. "You know this is what they'd want, don't you? And you know this is what you want. This is your home, Holly. This is your town, filled with your friends. It's where you belong."

Holly looked away from the sympathy in his eyes. "I don't know where my home is anymore, Quinn, and I don't know what they would have wanted."

"You do know. Deep down, under all that tough-woman front, you know that your sister would have wanted you to be around people who love you, and who could love their daughter. She would have wanted you to be in the house she thought was perfect for their little girl. She loved you, and she'd want you to be where you are loved."

"Please stop," Holly whispered, hating that he was bringing up thoughts that she tried so hard to keep at bay. "I can't talk about this," she said, sitting up. "Why do we have to talk about all this? Why can't we just enjoy each other's company?"

"Because I don't just want to make love to you. I want you—for the long haul. I want you and Ella. I want you to stay here and marry me."

Holly stopped breathing for the briefest of seconds. He couldn't mean it. But the truth was in every line of his face, in the glint of his eyes.

The rain pattered soothingly against the windows, and

the fireplace silently absorbed the dampness in the room. Holly didn't move as Quinn sat up and took her hand, raising it to his lips, kissing it until her breath quickened. The sheet was bunched around his waist, his torso bare. She took in the strong lines, the bronzed skin of his muscled chest and shoulders, the lines of his biceps clearly defined when he reached out to cup her face.

"Marry me," he said in a thick voice that made Holly's eyes fill with tears.

Marry me. She didn't move, didn't breathe, as his words stopped everything inside her. Holly wanted to say something. She wanted to tell him the truth, that she was scared. A few years ago, she would have said yes. She would have let him in and taken that leap of faith. But now…now, if she stayed here, she'd fall so completely and totally in love with Quinn, and she'd have this fairy-tale idea of happily-ever-after. And when it shattered, she wouldn't be able to pick up the pieces of herself again. She'd done that too many times, and every time she did, she came back a little less whole.

Holly shook her head. "I can't," she whispered.

"Why not?"

"Nothing lasts, and I couldn't recover—"

"Why wouldn't we last?" he asked, reaching out to touch her cheekbone, his thumb grazing her skin. She wanted to fold herself into him and not think about any of this.

"Can't we just spend the weekend together? I want to enjoy this, I want to enjoy us. Why do we have to talk about this now? Please, Quinn," she said, and breathed a sigh of relief as he leaned forward to capture her lips in a slow, gentle kiss.

"I just asked you to marry me, even though I swore I'd

never get married again. And now here I am putting myself out there, and you tell me let's just enjoy ourselves?"

Holly's eyes widened, and she tried her hardest not to cry.

"What happens when you leave?" she whispered.

Quinn frowned. "Leave?"

She nodded. "If things don't work—"

"I don't leave. I won't leave. Things will work."

"What about when something happens to you? I almost didn't make it when Jen and Rick died. I wanted to shrivel up in a ball and stay there forever. But I couldn't because I had Ella to take care of. But if I'm here, I'm going to grow closer and closer to you every day. And I'm going to start relying on you and depending on you. And loving you," she whispered, staring into his eyes. "If something happened to you, Quinn, I wouldn't survive."

Quinn's gut twisted painfully. Holly's eyes were wide, weary, her face drawn. He fought the urge to reach out and hold her, to destroy whatever demons she was afraid of. "Nothing is going to happen to me. Nothing is going to happen to you. Nothing is going to happen to Ella," he said forcefully, believing it with all he had. He needed her to believe it, too, before she ruined everything, before she shut him out.

"I have to go back," she whispered, and he knew she meant Toronto.

Quinn swallowed the curse in his mouth. He knew she was making a mistake. But he also knew she needed to be the one to figure that out. He nodded slowly and reached out to cup her face in his hands. "You waited ten years for me, Holly. I'll wait for you, for as long as it takes. I love you," he whispered.

Holly shook her head, then squeezed her eyes shut and rested her forehead on his chest. And when her arms slipped around him, her hands climbing his back, her nails digging into his skin, he physically tried to absorb her pain. Her head dipped down to just below his collarbone and hovered for a moment before he felt her mouth on his skin. Her hair tickled his chest and she began a slow, torturous descent with her lips and tongue.

"Come here," he implored, his hands firmly grasping her head, then her waist, lifting her on top of him, all his self control focused on filling her until she didn't feel empty, until she knew that he could make her whole again.

Chapter Ten

Quinn was on his way to buy Ella some cupcakes. Tomorrow night was the big reveal and birthday party, and he was dying to see her. He missed her. He missed her smile and her laugh. And he missed the way her little arms wrapped themselves around his neck, the way she reached out for his hand. And the way her faith in him made him feel whole again. He had convinced himself he wasn't worthy of having kids. He had blamed himself for so long, but now he was done. There was a little girl that he loved. He didn't know how it happened, but when he was busy letting his guard down, Ella had found a way to reach him. To her, he was good enough, he was worthy. And he wasn't going to let Holly derail everything they had.

He understood why she was pushing him away. But that wasn't good enough. Monday morning, after they'd made love, she'd shut down. But he'd known that was going to happen, he'd felt it when she clutched onto him in bed. When he'd walked out of her house that day, he had faith that she'd call. That was five days ago. He'd stayed away. He wasn't going to push her, because he wanted her to come to him on her own. The remaining house details were minor so he'd left Jake in charge.

But he missed Holly. She was stubborn, but he knew that what they had was one of a kind. Nights without her were torture. Days without her witty remarks and sexy smiles—even without her infuriating designer decisions—were tedious. Holly and Ella made him want to be the husband and father he now knew he was capable of being.

He had spent the morning in the city, buying Ella her birthday gift. He'd been a little stumped at first—but when he'd entered the handmade toy shop, he knew what he was going to buy as soon as he saw it. The enormous, pale green dollhouse was perfect. It was made out of wood, with authentic, hand-carved details, complete with white gingerbread trim. Quinn bought the house, the miniature furniture, and some little figurine family called the Smiths. He knew Ella was a little young for it, but he couldn't resist. And he had faith that in a couple of years, he'd be watching Ella play with it. And on his way out of the store, he took one look at the pink tool belt filled with children's tools and purchased that, too.

As he loaded all the stuff into the back of his truck, an antique jewelry store across the street caught his eye. He'd walked in there, knowing exactly what he wanted to do, what he should have done the moment Holly came back to town, really. Half an hour later, he was on his way back to Red River, with something for both of his girls.

It had been a last-minute idea to get Ella some cupcakes.

Quinn opened the door to the Water's Edge Bakery, and a waft of cinnamon and fresh coffee greeted him.

"Hey, Quinn," Natalia Waters, the owner of the bakery, called out.

"Hi, Nat, how are you?" He smiled, walking up to the counter. The place had a few patrons sipping coffees and eating, despite the lunch hour being over.

"Good. Busy getting ready for Holly's big party tomorrow night," she said while arranging cookies in a pink box. He forced himself to keep his smile relaxed at the mention of Holly as he stood in front of the display. His eyes immediately went to the assortment of cupcakes lit up behind the glass.

"Are you looking for something in particular?" Natalia asked.

"Yeah, uh, cupcakes actually," Quinn said, bending down to peer closer. There were pink ones with pink flowers, red ones with ladybugs, yellow ones with butterflies, and green ones with caterpillars. How was he supposed to know which one Ella would like best? And then another thought popped into his head. "Nat, are these cupcakes all-natural?"

She smiled and nodded. "Yup, even the food coloring."

"Hello, Quinn."

Quinn's body tensed and he slowly straightened to look at the owner of that smooth voice, even though he already knew.

"Hi, Christine," he said, clearing his throat.

"I never had you pegged as a cupcake eater," she said, smiling.

Quinn smiled back. "They're not for me. You're looking well." Christine was pretty in an

I'm-so-delicate-that-I-can't-even-stand-on-my-own-two-feet sort of way, very unlike the woman who had fallen off a ladder trying to prove how independent she was. She was tall, extremely thin, with, well, a rather disproportionately large head. It was absurd, but... Quinn blinked rapidly... Yes, she did resemble a lollipop. That ridiculous observation was thanks to Holly. But there was no way in hell he was going to admit that out loud to anyone. It was juvenile. Feminine. Pure Holly and Claire. He was embarrassed for even thinking about it.

"Thank you. You, too," she said primly. "So, who are the cupcakes for?"

Quinn caught a flash of purple and pineapples from the corner of his eye as Eunice Jacobs practically dove into one of the armchairs at the front of the bakery. It was amazing, for all the woman's bulk and age, that she could move so swiftly. "They're, uh, for Holly's niece," he said. Now that Christine was here, he was going to use this opportunity. He wanted closure.

"Chris, I'm sorry," he began, lowering his voice and turning away from the counter. He could tell she was startled. Before she could ask why, he continued. "I hate how we left things, and I want you to know that the way I treated you isn't something I'm proud of." It was done. The words were out, and he could finally move on with a clean slate.

• • •

Holly stared at her reflection in the floor-to-ceiling mirror in the newly accessorized en suite. She should look happier. She was about to host Ella's first birthday party and an open house. The renovation was officially over. Her colleagues were coming from Toronto, and then next week, she'd be packing up to resume her normally scheduled life. So why did the thought of returning to her condo in the city, her glamorous office at Martin Laurence, sound…horrifying? One word…or, one man: Quinn.

You waited ten years for me, Holly. I'll wait for you. For as long as it takes. Quinn's words and promises kept her up at night, wondering if there was a way they could be together. Could she take that leap of faith and stay here? Trust that she could have a happily-ever-after? He was so sure. He was certain they would last, that they would be safe. His faith tempted her. He had been right about a lot of things. Maybe he was right about this, too. In the last few days, Holly had picked up the phone so many times to call Martin and say she wasn't coming back. But then she'd slam the phone down and berate herself. What was she thinking? How could she just throw away years of hard work for…for a life that sounded too good to be true? Quinn made it sound so easy. She could stay here and raise Ella—with Quinn. They could be a real family. And what better home could there be than the one that she had grown up in? But the house was officially going on the market tonight. She'd already signed the listing papers. And she'd already said no to Quinn.

Holly ran a brush through her hair, leaving it loose around her shoulders. She took a deep breath and smoothed the front of her navy silk dress that fell to just below her knees. The scooped neckline revealed her collarbone, but the real wow factor was that the dress was backless. Her strappy navy heels made her legs look long and added just the right amount of sensuality. Her arms were bare except for a silver linked bracelet that her grandmother had given her years ago. She clasped her hooped silver earrings and touched up her hair once again as she looked at herself in the mirror.

This was the Holly she remembered, the Holly who had her life together. Sophisticated, fearless, smart. She hoped Martin and the others would remember that. She added a final spritz of perfume and made her way downstairs, lighting the white candles in various glass containers along the way. Having a bunch of interior designers over for the evening meant that the entire house would be on showcase and no details should be overlooked.

She entered the kitchen, where Claire was putting the finishing touches on a glorious bouquet of white calla lilies on the center island. Natalia and her crew were getting the finger foods ready and arranging the silver trays and crystal glasses. Fuchsia and lime green balloons were arranged in massive bouquets throughout the house.

"Claire, the flowers are gorgeous!" Holly exclaimed. Her friend looked up at her, beaming.

"Glad you like them! Speaking of gorgeous, you look beautiful, Holl," Claire said, leaning against the counter.

"Well, thanks, so do you," Holly said, smiling at her. Claire was stunning in a dark red dress that was a dramatic backdrop for her ivory skin and dark hair and eyes.

"Nat, all of this looks delicious."

"Thanks, Holly. This house is unbelievable. You are so talented," Natalia said, pausing from arranging the crystal stemware in rows on the countertops. The chandelier over the island added sparkle to the glasses.

"Thank you. I'm just happy that it's over. Being on this

side of a reno is a lot more difficult," she said, laughing. "It's hard not to get bogged down by all my personal preferences and remember the big picture. But we made it. I think I'm going to help myself to the wine," Holly said as she poured a glass. "Would you ladies like a glass?"

"No thanks, hon. I'm going to wait until all the flowers are where they should be," Claire said with a wink.

"Me neither. I don't trust myself. I'll wait until the end of the party," Nat said, then turned to give instructions to some of the servers.

"I thought Quinn would be here by now," Claire said curiously. Sometimes it was difficult having such a perceptive friend.

"I'm sure he'll be here soon." Holly pretended to arrange the already perfect stacks of white dishes on the island. She hadn't really figured out what she was going to say to him. Or what he'd say to her. And the thought of Quinn mingling with people in her Toronto life was…strange. And, of course, there was Daniel.

"Knowing Quinn, he probably bought an entire store full of toys for Ella," Claire continued.

Holly sighed.

"What have you done, Holly?"

"I think I'll go see if Ella is awake yet," Holly said, hoping she could distract her friend. "I bought her the cutest little pink dress and shoes." Holly's voice trailed off as Claire's frown deepened.

Claire raised her eyebrows. "Tell me."

"I told him I needed time and space," Holly mumbled, taking a sip of wine.

"You're not an astronaut," Claire snapped, then softened

her tone as she reached out to hug her. "Don't push him away. I know you're scared—"

"How does everyone know this about me?"

Claire didn't say anything for a few seconds, but Holly saw the sympathy steal across Claire's eyes. "Who wouldn't be, sweetie? You've been through hell and you've come out the other side, stronger. You're the best, Holl, and you deserve the best. You deserve to be happy."

Holly felt her heart pounding as the truth of what Claire was saying hit her. She stared at her a moment longer and knew that if she continued this conversation, she would end up in a pile of tears and an empty bottle of wine. A clatter of dishes brought her back to the present. "You know what, I can't think about this right now. I've got thirty designers coming over here, and my boss. I've got to stay focused. And it's Ella's birthday. I don't need to be thinking about Quinn tonight."

Claire sighed and shook her head. "Fine. You're not off the hook, though."

Holly smiled at her. "Thanks."

"I think I'm going to start drinking now," Claire said wryly and poured herself a large glass of wine.

Ella was the star of the party. She was lapping up all the attention being thrown on her, and she had people laughing out loud at her antics. The more they laughed, the more charming she became. Holly was smiling as Claire's parents fed Ella strawberries, and with each one that was placed in her mouth, Ella would reward them by clapping.

Holly's phone buzzed, and she tried to maintain a neutral expression on her face as she glanced down at another text message from one of her colleagues. Another cancellation. The only person from Toronto that had bothered to show up was Daniel. Even Martin had called earlier to say that he just couldn't get away. Holly tried not to take it personally, but it was pretty darn hard not to. They all knew it was Ella's birthday as well, and they knew the circumstances behind her adopting Ella. She would have thought they'd be genuinely interested in celebrating with her. This night wasn't just a birthday. It was a farewell to the most difficult and life-changing year of her life.

"Oh, Holly, what a beautiful job you've done with your grandparents' home," Mrs. Jacobs gushed as she nearly careened into Holly. Holly glanced down at the elderly woman's empty martini glass and stifled her grin at the thought that her grandmother's friend was getting tipsy. She fondly remembered Mrs. Jacobs coming to the house for tea and keeping her grandmother in stitches over her animated chit-chat. The woman was a notorious gossip, but Holly knew she had a heart of gold.

"Oh, thank you, Mrs. Jacobs," Holly said, smiling when the old woman squeezed her hand a little sloppily.

"They would be so proud of you for everything. And the way you've stepped in to raise your beautiful little niece," Mrs. Jacobs continued.

Mrs. Jacobs placed her hand on Holly's shoulder. "Your grandparents would be so happy to see you back here. To know that their house was going to be lived in by you and their great-granddaughter, well, it's just wonderful," she said, her voice shaking, her eyes tearing up.

It was as if she'd just punched Holly in the stomach. No one knew she was listing the house. She'd asked Sabrina to keep the sign off the lawn until next week. She hadn't wanted the birthday party to be overshadowed by the FOR SALE sign.

"I see Quinn Manning is here tonight," the elderly woman continued to speak. "Always so dashing, isn't he? I often thought you two would make an excellent pair, you know. I must say, I was surprised when I saw him and Christine together yesterday," Mrs. Jacobs said with a frown. Holly tried to ignore the immediate surge of jealousy and betrayal that hit her. It was ridiculous, of course. If there was one thing she knew about Quinn, it was that he wasn't a cheat. Besides, she had told him she was still leaving Red River, so she had no right to claim him as hers.

"Well, that's nice that they've kept in touch," Holly said, trying to make her voice sound as normal as possible. Knowing this conversation would only lead to more insecurity and gossip, Holly changed the subject. "Oh look, a fresh round of martinis," Holly said loudly, praying the woman would take the bait. It was her lucky night—Mrs. Jacobs followed the waiter across the room. She made a mental note to make sure someone drove Mrs. Jacobs home tonight.

Holly swallowed against the lump of unexpected emotion clogging her throat as she watched the woman depart. The entire night had been like this. People from her youth—townspeople, friends of her grandparents—all had comforting words to say to her, and offered lovely memories of what her grandparents had been like. She thought it would hurt. She thought that those memories and those people would bring her too much pain to deal with.

But instead, the memories of this town, of these people, of her family, had cocooned around her. She felt the safety and the warmth of people who cared about her.

Holly's eyes inevitably went to where Quinn was standing with his brothers. The three of them were so different, yet they all had an inherent decency about them. She had been trying to avoid Quinn all night. But he was a hard man to miss. Holly's eyes wandered over Quinn's face and body, undeniably handsome in a navy pullover and dark pants. She followed his gaze, and her heart stopped as his face stretched into a smile. He was staring at Ella.

"Hey, gorgeous," Daniel said from behind her.

Holly spun around to smile at the only friend from work who'd actually shown up. "I'm so glad you came," she said, giving him a big hug.

"I wouldn't miss it," he said, smiling at her.

"What happened to everyone?" Holly asked, not sure if she was mad or hurt.

"Deadline on the E Street condo project got bumped by two weeks, so everyone's scrambling," Daniel said. Holly knew what that meant—long nights, no life, and practically living at the office. It did make Holly feel a little better that she wasn't just being blown off.

"How are the Thorntons?" Holly asked, not feeling any of the insecurity she had felt before. Funny, because right now, the Thorntons seemed like the most insignificant people in the world to her. They dimmed in comparison to the people that filled this room.

Daniel rolled his eyes. "You were right—totally high-maintenance. But I'm not going to complain. I'll be on the West Coast for a few weeks, all expenses paid, so I guess it's worth it," he said, raising his eyebrows. "You did a gorgeous job on this house, sweetie," he gushed, looking around. "I snooped around the entire place. Great counters in the kitchen," he added, taking a sip of his drink.

"Thanks." Holly smiled.

"I bet you miss the city, eh? How are you surviving without your daily Starbucks fix? And that downtown—there's nothing there. It's like three blocks," he said, shaking his head.

Holly stifled her laugh. "There's a great bakery in town that makes the best lattes. It's actually quite nice."

Daniel didn't look as though he believed her. "You know, I had to stop in town for gas and people talked to me," he said, lifting his eyebrows.

Holly grinned. "What do you mean?"

"I mean, like strangers actually made conversation," he said, taking a drink of wine.

"Welcome to small-town life, Daniel."

"Yeah, and then some crazy old lady almost mowed me down in her Mini Cooper," he said.

Holly tried not to spit out her wine. She knew exactly who that woman was. "I missed you, Daniel." She laughed.

"Me, too. You know you're the only woman I'd drive to the sticks to see, don't you? I'll be happy if I don't hit a deer or something on my drive home tonight. Do you know there are no streetlights on these roads?"

Holly laughed again, and tried not to look over at Quinn.

• • •

"Quinn, unless you're planning on starting a fight, I suggest

you stop glaring at that guy," Jake said, popping an olive into his mouth.

Quinn ignored his brother and kept his eyes focused on the bony hand that was groping Holly.

"Looks like they're really close," Evan said, taking a sip of wine.

Quinn clenched his teeth so tight he thought he was in danger of dislocating his lower jaw. Listening to Jake and Evan's moronic play-by-play of Holly and Daniel was setting him on edge. As if he'd needed any help.

Jake reached for a smoked salmon bundle as a waiter passed by. "Holly really knows how to throw a party."

"Yeah, looks like practically the entire town is here," Evan said, looking around the packed room.

"Hey guys," Claire said as she walked over to stand beside them. Quinn gave her a quick smile, then went back to watching Holly, who had thrown back her head with laughter. *He was funny, too?*

"Hey, Claire," Evan said. "Who's the guy with Holly?"

Quinn could feel Claire's eyes on him while she answered, "That's Daniel."

Quinn's stomach churned and he studied him more closely. The guy had a big nose. And he was kind of bony looking. Anemic, maybe.

"They work together," Claire said, her voice sounding a bit strained.

"Really?" Evan asked.

Claire nodded. "Yeah. He's been her mentor since she started there, sort of took her under his wing."

"I'll bet," Jake said under his breath.

Quinn turned to glare at Jake. "What's that supposed to

mean?"

Jake shrugged. "All I'm saying is that Holly's hot, and he's been crawling all over her like an octopus."

"Don't worry, Quinn, I think he's gay," Evan said.

"He's not gay," Quinn and Claire spoke at the same time.

"And, I'm not worried," Quinn added.

"You sure? He's an interior designer, isn't he? And look at what he's wearing," Evan said.

Claire laughed. "What's wrong with what he's wearing?"

"Nothing. It's perfect. You don't own anything like that, Quinn."

"Thanks," he growled, shooting Evan a glare.

"You guys are horrible." Claire laughed. "Seriously, you're like a bunch of old hens."

"We're not hens. Men aren't hens," Jake growled.

This conversation had gone on far too long. "Don't you guys have anything better to do?"

His brothers shook their heads and Claire looked away quickly.

"Nope. This is my first night off in weeks," Evan said, motioning to a waiter for a refill.

"Seriously, Quinn, you could take that guy out," Jake said with a nudge.

Quinn refused to engage him.

"Jake, I highly doubt that beating him up would solve anything," Claire said.

"Trust me, it would solve a lot of problems. Quinn, I bet all it would take is two punches and he'd run home crying like a baby."

Quinn nodded, his fist clutched tightly by his side. He was thinking more like one punch would do it.

"Oh, Holly would love that," Claire said into her wine glass.

Quinn took a deep breath.

"Yeah, seriously, don't be taking Jake's advice or you'll wind up doing something you regret," Evan said in a low voice.

"Thanks, but I don't see you coming up with any brilliant ideas. Don't you have a life to save or something?"

"I already saved a half dozen or so, thanks," Evan said, shooting Jake a smug grin.

"Can you two shut up?" Quinn roared. He rolled his shoulders. He needed to regroup. Focus. He was acting like some sort of adolescent, macho, possessive boyfriend or something. "You're right, Claire." He forced himself to turn and give her a quick smile.

"Holly did a great job on this old place, didn't she? Her grandparents would have been thrilled. You and Jake did beautiful work here, too," Claire said.

"Thanks," Quinn said.

Jake plucked a martini off a moving silver tray and took a large gulp, ignoring Claire. Quinn shook his head. He didn't have time to address his brother's issues tonight.

Claire stared at Jake with a hurt expression on her face. Quinn watched incredulously as his brother pretended to concentrate on the olives in his glass. He had never seen Jake drink a martini—or anything that wasn't beer.

"Well, I better go see if they need any help with the cake," Claire said. Evan and Quinn said good-bye, while Jake downed the contents of his glass.

"What the hell is your problem, Jake?" Evan growled.

"What do you mean?" he mumbled.

"Did you suddenly lose all your brain cells? You can't drink a martini and hold a conversation?"

Jake shrugged and glared at him. Quinn let out a frustrated sigh. "Do you have a problem with Claire or something?"

"She just bugs me." Quinn watched as Jake clenched his jaw. He noticed, though, that Jake's eyes trailed her around the room as she approached Natalia and a group of friends. Quinn let the issue go. Getting inside of Jake's head was like falling into quicksand.

Despite the hurt Quinn felt over Holly's rejection, when he had walked into Holly's home tonight, he had been filled with pride over what she'd accomplished. Everything she had chosen for the house was perfect, and the attention to detail had been worth it. Even the countertops were right.

And then there was the woman herself. Her back had been turned to him when he'd walked in. Her gorgeous, smooth, soft, bare back in dark silk that clung to every inch of the body he knew so well. Desire had pumped through him involuntarily as he watched her move about, chatting with guests. Until he saw that man's skinny hand on her gorgeous bare back. Then, desire had quickly turned into jealousy. And he was not the jealous type.

But since Holly had come back into his life, he didn't know what "type" he was anymore. He had come here tonight hoping to make things right. He knew if he waited for her to come to him, he'd wait forever. And that wasn't an option.

• • •

"Holly, are we ready to sing 'Happy Birthday?'" Natalia asked her as she entered the kitchen.

Holly nodded. "Yes, now is perfect. I'll meet you in the dining room," she said, slowly making her way through the crowd. She tried to embrace the thought of Jennifer and Rick, and hoped she was doing justice to the celebration of the little girl they had adored. As Holly walked through the crowd alone, she ached for Quinn, for Ella, for herself. She hated that she was a coward. She was hiding from the only man she'd ever loved because she was a coward. She was hiding from her niece because she was a coward. And she was leaving Red River because she was a coward. That re-alization had slapped her across the face more than once tonight. And when she'd stared at Quinn, who'd been watching Ella from the other side of the room, she finally knew. She admitted to herself how important Quinn was—to her and to Ella.

"Holly!" Sabrina called out and motioned Holly to stand with her in a quiet corner.

"I'm glad you made it," Holly said, forcing a smile on her face as her Realtor held out a thick file.

"You're not going to believe this," Sabrina said, beaming. Holly's stomach turned. "What?"

"We have an offer! Full asking price," Sabrina said, holding up the file like a trophy.

"Pardon?" Holly whispered.

"Well, almost full asking," Sabrina said, with a brief frown. "Something about the purchaser wanting the seller to replace the basement windows. But those are all minor details we can discuss. I know tonight is crazy, but we've got twenty-four hours to respond. I'll give you a call in the morning. I just knew you'd want this news right away!" Sabrina said, and Holly forced herself to look happy.

"Sure. Thanks. I, um, if you'll excuse me, we're about to cut the cake," Holly mumbled, seeking out Ella in the crowd. It was wrong, it felt all wrong. If she were doing the right thing, she'd be ecstatic right now. It would mean she'd be able to go back to work right away. She'd be able to pick up her old life right where she'd left it. Except she wasn't the same woman she was when she came here. Coming back to Red River had changed her. She was stronger, and she knew what she wanted. Maybe she was a little late in figuring it out, but she knew what was right.

Claire's parents brought Ella over, and Holly looked at them, at Ella, and knew. Holly smiled and picked up Ella and held her close, breathing in her delicious scent. Her pink dress with the full skirt was already stained, and her little butterfly hair clips were dangling precariously, but she was Holly's little princess.

The lights dimmed and guests gathered around as Natalia walked into the room with a polka-dot, three-tiered, pink and green cake. And everyone broke out into a boisterous rendition of "Happy Birthday."

As Holly sang "Happy Birthday" to her niece and looked around the room at the familiar faces from her childhood, emotion began seeping through her. She sought Quinn, her eyes surveying the room, but she didn't see him. She sang the chorus along with everyone, smiling back at all the people she loved. But where was Quinn? He wouldn't have missed this moment, she knew that. Even if he was mad at her, he wouldn't have missed this for Ella. Ella snuggled her face deep onto Holly's shoulder, and she knew Ella must be overwhelmed with all the noise. Holly squeezed her closer and everyone clapped, the singing over.

Ella whispered, "Mama."

Everything inside Holly froze. She tried to breathe against the weight of the past that had been holding her prisoner for so long. As her little girl held on to her with the utmost faith, Holly finally found her faith and grasped it. This was her moment of truth, where fear had to depart or reign forever. She clutched Ella's head, her soft hair beneath her fingers, and willingly accepted what this little girl already knew.

Her knees felt weak and her eyes scanned the room relentlessly, desperately seeking Quinn, because he was the missing link. He was family. Holly backed up a step. And there he was. Hard wall at her back, hands on her shoulders, he ducked his head close.

"Come on, sweetheart," he whispered. Holly let Quinn lead them out of the room. As they walked up the stairs to Ella's room, Holly held on tighter to Quinn's strong hand, to Ella's small body. The little pink ballerina night-light greeted the three of them as they entered the room. Ella reached out for Quinn. He looked at Holly, and she attempted a smile as she handed her over.

"Hi, birthday girl," he whispered to Ella in a voice that was so soft and so endearing that it automatically made Holly smile. Holly stared through watery eyes at them, realizing she'd had a choice all along—she could let the memories of people from her past paralyze her, or she could embrace the people that were in her life now and make new memories. That is what Jennifer, Rick, and her grandparents would have wanted. They would have wanted Holly to have a family, and they would have wanted Ella to have a family.

She knew now that there would be no walking away from Quinn. He had her heart. And he had her daughter's heart.

"Ella called me 'mama,'" Holly whispered.

He smiled. "You are."

Holly nodded solemnly. She clasped her hands in front of her. She had to do this. He'd said he'd wait. So now it was her turn. "Quinn, someone put in an offer on the house."

Quinn's jaw clenched, his eyes going from her lips to her eyes. "And?"

"Full asking price."

He nodded. "They must really want it."

Holly frowned. "I guess. They mentioned something about those basement windows," she mumbled, quickly looking away. "But it must be some weirdo. I mean, who goes in at full asking on a house that has no competition?"

She looked up at him. Ella was snuggled in his arms, and he was just grinning at her. "It was probably a really smart person. Someone who knew the quality of the renovation, someone who understands the importance of a sound base-ment. So what are you going to do?"

"Rip up the offer and live here," she said, her eyes filling with tears as Ella lifted her head and smiled alongside him.

"That's good, because I'm the idiot who offered full asking," he said, laughing as he bent down to kiss her mouth.

"What?"

He nodded. She was torn between laughing and yelling at him. The boyish grin, the unruly strand of dark hair on his forehead, but mostly, mostly it was the pure, unadulterated love that was shining from his dark blue eyes that made her

smile. She was done with fear. She was going to let herself be loved. But first, there were a few unresolved issues she was curious about.

"I heard you had lunch with Christine," Holly said, crossing her arms.

Quinn rolled his eyes. "Mrs. Jacobs?"

Holly nodded, smiling.

"Jealous?"

Holly shook her head, still smiling.

"I needed closure," he said gruffly, reaching out to trace his thumb along her lower lip.

"And everything went okay?" she asked, trying to concentrate on the conversation and not the sensations his touch evoked.

"It did."

"So, is that job offer still available?" Holly asked, stepping closer to him.

A slow, sexy smile made its way across his face. "You're going to take the position?"

She nodded. "I feel kind of weird, considering—"

"We're sleeping together?"

She frowned at him. "Yeah. That's one way of putting it. I just know that everyone is going to think the only reason I got the job is because of our relationship."

"Holly, your reputation precedes you. It's not like you've never worked before and I'm just giving you this job."

She looked away for a moment, then nodded. "There's something else."

"Go ahead, what?"

"I think I'm going to have a hard time taking directions from you."

He threw his head back and laughed. And then, of course, so did Ella. "Don't worry, someone else heads up that section of our company."

"And I don't want to just be the woman you're sleeping with."

The moment went from laughter to tense silence. "What do you want, then?"

"I want to marry you."

Epilogue

Holly looked up from her computer screen in her newly completed, third-floor home office. It had been decorated with her favorite black and white toile wallpaper. Quinn had installed the white wainscoting and window seat. There was a play area for Ella, complete with the adorable green dollhouse Quinn had bought her. She smiled, a smile that, before Quinn and Ella came into her life, she wouldn't have been capable of. She stared for a moment at the view of the snowy landscape surrounding the house as she heard Ella's peel of laughter, followed by Quinn's deep chuckle.

Her grandparents would have been proud. The sad, old house had been once again made into a joyous family home. Their great-granddaughter was alive and blossoming. Their granddaughter had found love, a love as powerful, strong, and complete as the one they had shared. Jennifer and Rick would have been so happy to see their daughter. And day by day, Holly was able to think of Jennifer again. She saw her sister in Ella's laugh, in Ella's eyes. And every night when they put Ella to bed, Holly said good night to her sister, too.

She took a deep breath, admiring the glorious, platinum, antique diamond ring Quinn had given her, and let her eyes wander over the wall filled with photographs of the people they loved. Holly had decided that since she'd be spending lots of time up here, they needed to embrace the people who were in their lives now as well as those who were no longer with them. Pictures of Jennifer and Holly as girls, pictures of Jennifer and Rick, their grandparents, and Quinn's parents hung with pride. One day, when Ella was old enough, Holly would tell her everything about them. For now, they were a reminder to Holly, something she'd learned on her darkest days, that even though she loved people and lost them, as long as she was open to love, she would never be alone.

Quinn's footsteps traveled up the third-floor staircase and Holly smiled, flipping the lid closed on her laptop. The antique drafting table sat by the window, her red bag with the "Holly and Quinn" embroidery sitting atop it. Her heart swelled as the sight of the two most precious people in the world to her appeared in the doorway.

Quinn was holding a babbling, pink pajama-wearing Ella in his arms. She looked warm and cozy, while *he*, as he usually did after bath time, looked drenched and exhausted.

"Hi there," Quinn said, giving her a smile that still gave her goose bumps.

"Hi, you two. Ready for bed?" she asked, coming around from her desk to pick up Ella.

"You bet," Quinn said with a mischievous grin.

Holly laughed as the three of them made their way to Ella's bedroom. Holly and Quinn gave Ella a good-night kiss and placed their eighteen-month-old daughter in her crib. Holly wound the music box and Quinn turned off the light. Once the door was shut, Quinn tugged on Holly's hand and pulled her into their bedroom, closing the door behind them.

"Holly?" he asked, his tone serious but his eyes sparkling, as he drew her against him.

"Yeah?" she said, looking into his eyes, her heart racing as his strong arms held her close.

"Would this be a good time for a little confession?"

Holly's eyes narrowed, trying to decipher the expression on his handsome face. "As good as any."

"That attic was filled with mice. Like, an entire city block worth of mice."

Holly stared into his eyes, trying to keep a straight face. "I'm not scared of the mice anymore."

Quinn's eyes glittered. "You've made all my fantasies come true," he said, bending down and kissing her neck.

"Fantasies?" Holly whispered as he continued his sweet torment up to her lips, his words reminding her of the first kiss that had started everything.

"Oh, yeah, real hot fantasies." Quinn smiled as he carried her into his fantasy.

About the Author

Victoria James always knew she wanted to be a writer, and in grade five, she penned her first story, bound it (with staples) and a cardboard cover, and did all the illustrations herself. Luckily, this book will never see the light of day again. In high school she fell in love with historical romance, and then contemporary romance. After graduating University with an English Literature degree, Victoria pursued a degree in Interior Design and then opened her own business. After her first child, Victoria knew it was time to fulfill the dream of writing romantic fiction. Victoria is a hopeless romantic who is living her dream, penning happily-ever-afters for her characters in between managing kids and the family business. Writing on a laptop in the middle of the country in a rambling old Victorian house would be ideal, but she's quite content living in suburbia with her husband, their two young children, and a very bad cat. Victoria loves connecting with readers, and you can find her online at www.victoriajames.ca and on Twitter: @vicjames101.

Also by Victoria James

THE DOCTOR'S FAKE FIANCÉE
a Red River novel

THE BEST MAN'S BABY
a Red River novel

THE RANCHER'S SECOND CHANCE
a Passion Creek novel

THE BILLIONAIRE'S CHRISTMAS BABY

CPSIA information can be obtained
at www.ICGtesting.com
Printed in the USA
BVHW040246250920
589621BV00021B/544

9 781502 813794